Ghosts

A SYNDICATES NOVEL

R.G. ANGEL

R.G. ANGEL

DEDICATION

First to Zsuzsanna, without whom you would have never read Ghosts. Her not-so-passive harassment worked, and I owe her my sincerest gratitude.

To all of Jiro's fans, I hope his story ignites your desires and leaves you breathless for more. Your passion and support set my pages on fire, and I can't wait to fan the flames even higher.

R.G. ANGEL

PROLOGUE

Jiro

"Why can't you just stay, Jiro?" Anna's voice, usually so soft, was edged with desperation. "Why can't you choose me?"

The weight of Anna's words resonated in the silence,

echoing against the walls of her tiny campus apartment. Soft raindrops streaked down the windowpane, their rhythm contrasting sharply with our heated words.

It was a place where we managed to love each other in semisecrecy, but tonight, it felt like a battlefield. "I was born into this destiny, Anna. I was only here a few months because it was my orders, my mission. This life I've known, this path alongside Hoka… it's not a choice."

Her piercing blue eyes, usually so full of love and mischief, now bore into me with accusation and pain. "If you truly loved me, you'd find a way."

A bitter chuckle escaped my lips as I shook my head with frustration. "This isn't about love. It never was. I've been transparent about who I am and where I come from. There's nothing stopping you from joining *me* after you're done here."

She took a deep breath, her voice quivering. "I don't want that life, Jiro. I don't want to live in fear, always waiting for something bad to happen."

Feeling the weight of her words, I whispered bitterly, more to myself than her, "Hoka warned me… said outsiders can't understand. They never do."

Without another word, Anna turned, grabbed her coat, and stormed out. The door slammed behind her, and the finality of the sound urged me to action. Racing after her, I found myself on the streets, rain drenching my hair and clothes. I reached out, grabbed her arm and pulled her aside. "Anna! We can figure this out."

But our moment was shattered by the screech of tires. Time slowed. A car approached, its windows rolling down to reveal a shadowy figure, a gun gleaming menacingly.

"No!" I yelled, pushing Anna behind me.

Pain exploded through my side as a bullet found its mark. The wet street rushed up to meet me as I fell, the world dimming. Through the haze of pain and rain, my last thought was of Anna and the cruel twist of fate that brought us to this moment.

I forced my eyelids open, the weight of them almost unbearable, and through the blinding rain, a sight more heart-wrenching than my own pain met me: Anna, her usually vibrant blue eyes now dim and lifeless, lay a few feet away.

"Anna…" I whispered, every ounce of strength left in me propelling my body to crawl closer to her. Each movement sent searing pain through me, but the need to reach her overcame it all.

Finally, beside her, I cradled her lifeless form, pressing my face into her wet hair, tears mixing with the rain. "Anna, no, baby, please don't leave me," I begged, my voice hoarse and broken.

The cold rain on my skin, the metallic taste of blood in my mouth, none of it compared to the agony that tore through my heart. She wasn't supposed to be the victim. This wasn't how our story was meant to end.

Tears streamed down my face as I held her close, wishing I could trade places, that my life could be the one to fade while she continued on. But wishes didn't mend broken hearts, and they certainly couldn't bring back the dead.

My vision began to blur, the pain and blood loss taking

its toll. "I'm so sorry, Anna," I murmured, clutching her to me. Closing my eyes, I silently willed death to take me too, to reunite us somewhere beyond the pain and anguish of this moment.

The sirens in the distance grew louder, but they sounded so far away as if they were echoing from another lifetime. Their wailing blended with the anguished cries in my heart, an orchestra of torment.

A familiar voice called my name… Hoka, but my eyes were too heavy. Suddenly, I felt hands, strong and urgent, pulling me away from Anna's lifeless form. I fought against them, wanting nothing more than to stay by her side, but they persisted, prying me from the only thing that mattered.

I was loaded into an ambulance, voices and medical jargon surrounding me, but they felt distant, mere background noise. The only clarity that remained was Anna's face, her lifeless eyes, and the gut-wrenching weight of guilt.

Weeks turned into months. As my physical wounds began to heal, the emotional ones only deepened. Every mirror was a reminder of the life I had lost, every heartbeat a cruel reminder that I was still here and she wasn't.

I wished for amnesia, for any respite from the all-consuming guilt and pain. But life was unforgiving. It gave me memories that were both a curse and a blessing—memories of our love, our fights, our passion, and that last fateful day.

My journey became one of redemption and seeking forgiveness, not from the world, but from the silent ghost that lingered in my heart: Anna.

But how does one seek forgiveness from the one they

failed so utterly? That question haunted my every waking moment.

ONE

Jiro

Twelve years later.

Ghosts.

They filled my head, my life, and my
decisions. This past was haunting me and
influencing me far more than I thought.

I'd almost caused the irreparable and destroyed the life of the person I cared about the most, my best friend, my soul brother, and the head of the yakuza, Hoka Nishimura.

I had no other choice but to sacrifice the little peace I had left by my best friend's side to right some of my wrongs, but I was not sure it was enough, not when my actions revealed how haunted I was and how skewed my vision was, and I knew I had to start with my first true haunting moment.

I shook my head, trying to forget about Hoka for a few minutes as I opened the crooked side gates and followed the path up to her.

I stopped in front of the well-kept pink granite headstone.

Anna Myers, daughter, sister, friend. Gone too soon, but never forgotten.

Gone too soon... She was fucking *nineteen*. It was a tragedy, and it was all on my head.

"Hi, Anna," I whispered as the pain I felt restricted my lungs, preventing me from breathing right. I'd almost condemned Hoka to the same life of bitter regrets I live every day, where every breath was a striking reminder that I was still there when she wasn't.

I kneeled on the dry grass and adjusted my sunglasses. I'd never spent much time in Washington state, but I was pretty sure that sunny days were rare. Was it her way of welcoming me here?

"I'm sorry I didn't visit often. I..." I cleared my throat. "I was not welcome." That was the understatement of the century. Hoka had told me not to go to her funeral, but I loved her, and I wanted to say goodbye, which ended up in a full-on brawl with Leo, her twin brother.

It was the first time I'd let someone hit me; I hoped that each of the blows Leo landed would ease the pain in my heart and soul, but it didn't. If anything, it only made it worse, and I hated spoiling her funeral. I hated how people looked at me and how some of them probably thought it was partly her fault for being involved with someone like me.

I just looked at her grave for a few seconds, not really sure what I could say. I came here on an impulse after leaving Hoka's side, realizing that despite over ten years passing by, I was still very much influenced in my decisions by her death.

"I have countless deaths on my soul, you know. Some from even before we met, but none of them, none, weigh on me the way yours does." I took a deep breath, suddenly feeling so much older than I was. The weariness was anchored deep in my bones, and once again, I felt a flash of anger toward Hoka for saving my life instead of leaving me to bleed out on the street beside her.

"I'm not sure why I came," I admitted, resting my hand on the cool, soft surface. "I can't ask you for forgiveness, and I wouldn't want you to give it to me. I don't deserve it, but, Anna, despite how unfair it is, I need to make it right in some way. I need to…" I could feel my eyes prickle with unwanted tears. I'd cried a total of three times in my life.

The first time was when my mother passed away when I was four. The second was during a dumb game with Hoka when I fell out of a tree and broke my arm and leg at age eight. And the last time had been when I woke up from my injury to discover that my Anna was dead… I was twenty-two.

I swallowed hard through the lump of sorrow. I did not deserve that sorrow, the sadness—I didn't deserve to express it or feel better, not when I'd cut her life short. A life so full of potential and unaccomplished dreams.

I didn't deserve the relief, the atonement of these sins, and yet this was exactly why I was here.

It was ridiculous, really; I knew that. It was not like she could just appear and tell me what to do to right my wrongs *if it was even possible*.

How could you ever make amends for taking the life of an innocent? How could you…

"I can't believe you're here."

I tensed at the feminine, raspy voice behind me. The voice carried a certain relief, showing it couldn't be for me.

Who would be relieved to see me here? Kneeling on the grave of the woman I'd unwittingly killed. I may not have fired the gun that killed her, but it was just like I had. She'd no business being in my world, and I took her all the same.

"Jiro?" I kept my eyes on the grave despite hearing my name. It could only be one person, the only person who didn't judge me or hate me despite her pain of losing Anna.

I was unsure if it had been due to how young she'd been at the time, just a child really, or because she had the same infinite goodness as her sister.

"Please." Her voice broke, and I had no choice but to face her.

I turned my head to the side slowly, and I connected with a pair of light-purple Doc Martens boots. I let my eyes trail up bare calves to a fifties-style black dress with lilac hearts.

I continued until I reached her face and her wavy lilac hair drifting in the cool wind. I let out a sigh of relief, realizing she looked nothing like Anna.

"Hope," I acknowledged as I took in her features in more detail. She was still as colorful as she had been as a child, but she was not a child anymore; she was a woman—a young woman whom I had no business looking at.

"You remember me?" she asked with incredulity as if it were impossible.

How would I ever forget her? She'd been nothing less than a ray of sunshine. Hope… I'd never seen a name fit a person as well as it did her, even when she was a ten-year-old kid.

How old was she now? Twenty-two? Twenty-three?

"God answered my prayers," she said, letting out a tearless sob.

I frowned, finally looking at her blue eyes. The only things that were too similar to Anna for my comfort were rimmed red. She'd been crying—why had she been crying?

I felt the avenging monster in me rear its ugly head—asking to burn and destroy whoever put these tears in her eyes like we had any right to.

For all I knew, she could still be crying for her sister, and the only person I would have to destroy was me.

"I'm not a gift from God, Hope. I'm not the answer to any prayer."

"Yes, you are," she insisted. "I prayed for help, for a warrior to help me, and you came. I thought you forgot about us, but after all these years—you came."

I pursed my lips at the involuntary blow her tirade caused.

Forget? How could I ever forget when Anna's lifeless eyes were still so fresh in my mind? When I sometimes woke up in the morning hearing her last breath leave her body. I could never forget, and I would not want to.

"I need your help, Jiro, please. Leo got himself into something bad, and he's gone." She shook her head, resting her trembling hand on her mouth. "I can't involve the police, it's... complicated. I need someone like you. No, I need *you*."

I turned back toward Anna's grave. *Is this it? Is this what you want me to do? Save your twin brother?*

I nodded and stood up, realizing how tiny Hope really was.

Damn it, she could not be over five feet tall.

I took a deep breath and adjusted my leather jacket.

"Okay, tell me everything."

Two

Hope

Jiro Saito

I kept glancing at him as he stood in line at the café across from the cemetery, and I settled at the table he'd pointed to silently when we'd entered. Part of me couldn't help but think he was a figment of my imagination. The sight of Jiro crossing the gate of the cemetery as I gazed out of the bus window felt like a surreal moment, as if fate had intervened in my life to bring him to my small town. Just when I needed help the most. The timing was perfect, even a little too perfect, and I was not used to fate benefiting me… ever. So, I could not help but expect the penny to drop.

I glanced at him again, half expecting him to have vanished, but he was still there, glaring at the blackboard, listing the many, many coffee choices as if they had offended him.

I also could not help but notice the lingering looks from the soccer moms who were meeting there before going to pick up their kids at school. I felt a hint of irritation at the coveted looks they were giving him and wanted to slap myself for this. Who could blame them, though? He was a spectacular specimen of a man, tall, broad, and edgy, with tattoos peeking from the edge of his collar.

I shook my head and texted my boss, Max, telling him I would be very late or probably wouldn't make it at all. Still, I knew he wouldn't mind because no matter how weird my job was, at least I had a great boss who understood that my family drama sometimes required me to bail at short notice. It was probably why I was still working in this "temporary" job four years later.

Sighing, I put my phone down just as Jiro walked to the table with the two cups and the scowl still very much present on his face.

Was this his default mode? Probably.

"Did the coffee offend you?" I asked as he put the cups

on the table and took his seat across from me.

"Who needs that much choice?" he grumbled, taking his seat across from me. "Fuck, the woman in front of me seemed to recite the Pledge of Allegiance. Venti whip, soy tiramisu latte, chilled with two percent cream? What the fuck is that? I should thank you for ordering a plain latte." He removed his jacket to rest it on the back of his chair, and I couldn't stop myself from ogling at his shirt stretched across his chest, his muscled arms full of tattoos, and his wide, powerful hands.

"…start."

As I snapped out of my daze, I realized I had been caught red-handed ogling at the man's impressive physique. Feeling a wave of embarrassment wash over me, my cheeks turned crimson. I quickly composed myself and tried to regain my focus on the important matters at hand.

"Sorry?" I stammered, hoping to conceal my momentary lapse in concentration.

Jiro brought his cup to his lips, taking a sip as he maintained eye contact with me with his piercing dark eyes. He didn't speak, and with each passing second, I found myself fidgeting with the hem of my dress, avoiding his gaze.

Finally, he lowered his cup and spoke in a calm yet slightly amused tone. "I said, tell me everything from the beginning."

"Oh yes," I let out an uncomfortable smile. "I… I'm not even sure where to start." I hesitated, my fingers unconsciously tracing the faded scar on my arm, a bitter reminder of one of the many misfortunes from the past decade that had started with the heart-wrenching loss of Anna, but I didn't want to burden him with all that. He had enough guilt over his head, and I noticed how deeply anchored it still was as I saw him hunched over my sister's grave.

He tilted his head, his eyes narrowing slightly as he studied me. "What's got you so concerned about Leo?"

Ah, Leo, yes.

"I… for the past few years, he's been running with a dodgy crowd." I winced; it was quite a ride to hell, to be more accurate.

"I didn't expect that," Jiro replied calmly. "As I remember him, he was a star baseball player making varsity in his first year of college."

I nodded. "Yeah, that was before."

Jiro's eyes flashed with pain as his body tensed as if the mere remindcr of my sister's death caused him a physical blow.

He looked down at his black coffee cup, tapping his finger on the rim. "That was before I came in and destroyed all of your lives."

I sighed, leaning back on my chair. "It would be easy to blame it all on you, and I think Leo used you as an excuse, but—" I waved my hand dismissively. "There's no real excuse. He wanted revenge, he wanted quick money, he wanted…" *He wanted to die.* I added to myself. "I think he enjoyed that life, to be honest. It was easy money, easy everything, but he always came home. Always."

"And suddenly he didn't?"

As I shook my head, I felt the sting of tears welling up in

my eyes, threatening to spill over. Leo and I had never truly been close. The vast age difference and the self-destructive patterns that consumed him had created an insurmountable barrier between us. Grief didn't bring us closer together; it tore us apart… all of us.

"He's been a little more erratic these past few weeks. Worried, fidgety, but I thought it was just the money again." It was always the money. "And then a week ago, he left for work and never came back."

"Why didn't you call the police?"

"Would you?" I countered, my tone laced with a hint of challenge.

A half smile appeared on his face. "Touché, but your brother is not an executioner for the yakuza. He's a thirtysomething white boy who made poor life decisions."

As his words settled within me, a shiver ran down my spine, sending a surge of adrenaline through my veins. It wasn't fear that gripped me, as it should have for any rational person faced with such casual revelation. Instead, it was a twisted thrill, a strange sense of exhilaration at sitting with such a dangerous man doing something as boringly mundane as having a coffee at the local coffee shop.

Maybe, I thought to myself, I, too, possessed that reckless gene that seemed to be present in my family.

"The thing is," I began, glancing cautiously around the café to ensure our conversation remained private. We were sitting at a table far enough at the back to be out of earshot, and it dawned on me that Jiro had likely selected it for precisely that reason. "These people we're dealing with," I continued, my voice hushed but filled with a sense of urgency, "they're dangerous. If I were to call the police, I fear that…" My words trailed off, the weight of unspoken implications hanging heavily in the air. I couldn't bring myself to vocalize the potential danger I would put not only myself but also my sick mother in should they find out I talked to the authorities.

A wave of discomfort washed over me, accompanied by the lingering question of whether Jiro viewed me as a coward for prioritizing the safety of my family. Did he see me as someone who would cower in fear? The weight of that uncertainty gnawed at me, adding to the mounting pressures of the situation.

Just as I was lost in my thoughts, I was startled when Jiro's warm hand gently rested on top of mine. The touch sent a surge of electricity through my arm, causing goose bumps to rise on my skin. I couldn't deny the effect it had on me, even as I tried to maintain a composed exterior. How could such a simple, innocent gesture stir up such intense emotions within me? I reminded myself that I was not a naive ten-year-old girl harboring a crush on her sister's silent boyfriend. I was a twenty-two-year-old woman worried about her brother's safety.

I looked up, meeting his dark eyes full of understanding.

"You're right," he agreed, nodding in acknowledgment. "Involving the police at this stage would only escalate the situation and put us at further risk." Jiro's hand gently squeezed mine before releasing it, leaving behind a lingering warmth that continued to tingle on my skin. His next words carried a weight of determination and grim reality. "I will help you find him or, at the very least, uncover the answers you seek," he said, his voice filled with a somber resolve. The unspoken truth hung heavy between us—there was no guarantee that Leo was still alive. The thought sent a pang of sorrow through my heart, but I couldn't afford to dwell on it. Not yet.

Gratitude welled up inside me, and I let out a sigh of relief. "Thank you, Jiro. Thank you so much!"

He shrugged as if his offer was a given. "It's the least I can do after… everything," he said, his tone tinged with a hint of regret.

I opened my mouth to object, to assure him that none of this was his fault, that he didn't owe us anything. But he spoke before I could utter a word, effectively silencing any potential argument from me.

"Do you have any idea who your brother was working with?" Jiro inquired, his gaze steadily fixed on me.

I paused, gathering my thoughts. "I have some leads," I confessed, my voice tinged with determination and uncertainty. "Leo was secretive about his dealings, but I saw him with a couple of guys from the Mexican cartel, and one of them sometimes came to my work, trying to pick me up." I rolled my eyes mockingly but sobered up at the murderous scowl on Jiro's face.

"Do not get involved with them," he stated with a harshness that caught me off guard.

My brows furrowed in response, and I couldn't help but feel a surge of indignation. Regardless of any lingering childhood crush, I wasn't about to tolerate being spoken to in such a commanding tone.

"I have no intention of getting involved with any of

them, but I don't need your permission or approval for my actions," I asserted, raising my chin defiantly.

He raised his hands in surrender. "Look," he began, his voice softer now, "I'm sorry for coming across as controlling. I just—" He sighed and shook his head. "You're right. It was not my place."

His sincerity was obvious in his eyes, and I felt a flicker of understanding. Perhaps his overprotectiveness was born from his own experiences with Anna and the scars they had left.

I shook my head. "I'm sorry, too. I'm just worried and tired."

He nodded. "It's fine. I understand that worrying for the people you love can take a toll on you." He swiftly turned and retrieved his leather jacket, the gesture signaling his readiness to act. "Come on, let's go to your house. I want to have a look at your brother's room," he declared, his tone determined.

I hesitated for a moment, knowing that I had already scoured every inch of Leo's room, finding no substantial leads. "There's nothing to find in there. I've looked everywhere."

A knowing smile curved his lips, and his gaze locked with mine. "Trust me, Hope. You haven't searched the way I do," he assured me, his confidence unwavering. There was an air of mystery surrounding Jiro, a sense that he possessed knowledge and skills beyond my comprehension. In that moment, I couldn't help but feel a glimmer of hope reignite within me.

As we stepped out of the coffee shop, a gust of wind

brushed against my skin, making me shiver despite the thinness of my jacket.

He threw me a concerned look as if he hadn't missed my shiver. I doubted he missed much. "Where's your car?"

I fumbled with my words, feeling a hint of embarrassment creeping up within me. "I... I don't have one," I admitted, my voice softening. "I rely on the bus for transportation."

His eyebrows arched in mild astonishment, his expression silently questioning my lack of a vehicle. I shifted uncomfortably, a mix of self-consciousness and frustration brewing within me. Why was I letting something beyond my control make me feel inadequate?

"Should I be ashamed of that or something?" I asked, a touch of defensiveness slipping into my tone.

He immediately shook his head, his denial swift and genuine. "No! Of course not," he reassured me, his voice carrying sincerity. "I didn't mean it that way. It's just I remember you going on and on about one day being sixteen, buying your own car, and driving down the coast to San Diego," he reminded me, a flicker of nostalgia in his eyes.

A surge of warmth spread through my chest as I processed his words. "You remember that?" I asked, my voice filled with awe.

A small smile tugged at the corners of his lips, and he nodded. "Yeah, I remember," he replied, his voice charged with fondness and wistfulness. "You were so passionate about it, and I admired that. Life has a way of changing our plans, though."

If only he knew how right he was. Nothing from that little girl had remained after this decade, no matter how hard I tried to hold on to it.

He pointed toward a gray-and-black bike parked near the entrance of the cemetery. "I've got a spare helmet."

My eyes widened in surprise. "You have a bike?"

A mischievous glint danced in his eyes as he looked at me, one eyebrow arched. "Is Hope Myers scared?" he teased.

I straightened my posture, determined not to let any fear show. "No, of course not," I replied, my voice laced with determination.

"Good, let's go," he said, confidently striding across the street. With each of his long strides, I scrambled to keep up, my feet carrying me as quickly as they could.

As I caught up with him, my heart pounding with both excitement and trepidation, I couldn't help but feel a surge of adrenaline coursing through my veins. The prospect of riding on the back of his bike, the wind whipping against my face, and my body pressed against his was both exhilarating and nerve-racking. But I knew I had to push past any hesitations. Leo's safety and finding the truth were at stake.

Jiro extended the helmet to me, and I hesitated for a moment before encircling it with my arms. Taking a deep breath, I knew it was time to reveal the painful truth about how our lives had taken a turn for the worse.

"I… ummm… We're not living in the house," I finally admitted, my voice wavering slightly. Avoiding eye contact, I fidgeted on my feet as if searching for something on the street to distract myself. "We sold it a few years back." The painful truth lingered in my mind—I knew deep down that we had lost it to the bank. "We're now renting a place on

Rendall Close."

"Hope, look at me, please," Jiro asked, his voice gentle yet insistent.

Reluctantly, I turned my gaze toward him, hoping that my face didn't betray the depths of my struggles.

"What happened?" he asked, his eyes shining with concern. I didn't want him to pity me. I could accept a lot but not pity.

I shrugged, attempting to brush off the weight of the question, shielding myself from the vulnerability that threatened to consume me. "It was too big," I replied, my words lacking conviction.

The furrow in Jiro's brow deepened, his doubt evident. I silently thanked whatever forces may be that he didn't press for further details. The truth was too much to reveal now in the middle of the street after just seeing him again after more than a decade.

Without another word, Jiro started his bike, the engine revving to life with a low growl. He reached for his phone, a determined expression on his face. "What's the address?" he asked, his voice resolute.

I hesitated, a knot of unease forming in my stomach. Revealing our current address meant exposing the harsh reality of our circumstances, the descent into a neighborhood plagued by crime and despair. It would be difficult to hide the extent of our struggles from Jiro, and I wasn't sure if I was ready to bear that vulnerability or add to his already misplaced guilt.

Taking a deep breath, I realized I had no choice if I wanted a chance to ever find Leo.

"It's eleven thirty-four Rendall Close," I replied with resignation.

Jiro typed the address into his phone, his fingers moving swiftly across the screen. In that moment, it felt like someone had lifted a weight off my shoulders. As if I had finally taken the first step to finding my brother and unraveling the truth. He glanced at me briefly, his expression unreadable, and jerked his head for me to hop on his bike.

I put on the helmet, secured it on my head, and then climbed onto the back of the bike, wrapping my arms tightly around Jiro's waist. The solidness of his body provided a sense of security, and I allowed myself to lean on him, both physically and emotionally. In that moment, I realized how much I had longed for support and someone to lean on all these years.

As we set off once again, the wind whipping against my face, I couldn't help but feel a renewed sense of courage. With Jiro by my side, I knew I didn't have to face the uncertainties alone.

As the scenery blurred past us, I held on tightly to Jiro, trusting him to guide us through the twists and turns. The rumble of the engine and the rush of adrenaline fueled my resolve. Together, we would find my brother and maybe even confront the ghosts of our past.

THREE

Jiro

I had spent years honing my ability to read people, a skill that came with my position as Hoka's right hand and enforcer. It was essential for me to discern guilt and innocence, to make decisions that would determine fates. But my training also allowed me to recognize pain and to sense the hidden turmoil within individuals.

As I sat across from her at the table, meeting her troubled blue eyes, I had seen beyond the facade she tried to maintain. It was clear to me that her situation was far worse than she let on. There was a weight in her gaze, a subtle vulnerability that betrayed the magnitude of her struggles.

She may have shrugged off my questions, deflecting with vague answers, but I knew there was much more beneath the surface. It was in the way she fidgeted, avoiding eye contact, and in the unspoken words that hung heavy in the air between us.

I had become accustomed to dealing with darkness and navigating the shadows of society, but there was something about her that struck a chord within me. A sense of empathy welled up inside, an urge to protect and understand her. I should not feel that protective of her; I couldn't afford to make the same mistake twice. Anna's association with me had sealed her fate, and I couldn't allow history to repeat itself with her sister.

Even if I hadn't suspected her financial situation, I would have as I stopped my bike in front of such a decrepit building that it made Violet's previous place look like the Hilton.

"It's temporary," she said, her voice tinged with embarrassment as her cheeks flushed with color. I knew she was trying to downplay the situation, to assure me it wasn't as bad as it seemed. But the truth was hard to ignore.

I nodded, even though I had my doubts about the temporary nature of her living arrangement. There was an air of desperation about her, a vulnerability that belied her attempts to maintain a brave front. She deserved better than this, and I couldn't help but feel a sense of responsibility to help her find a safer and more stable environment.

"Thank you for helping me…" she trailed off, her voice filled with a mix of gratitude and hesitation. I could see the turmoil in her eyes as she glanced at the run-down building, her expression pained. But before she could say anything further, she abruptly changed the subject, "Let's go."

We walked down the path; her steps hurried and stiff. I recognized that walk—the one taken when summoning the courage to face a difficult situation. It struck me how she seemed determined to keep up a facade as if she believed I would judge her. The truth was, I could never condemn her for the hardships she faced.

Despite her attempts to shield me from her struggles, I couldn't help but question how her life had taken such a drastic turn. It didn't make sense that her family's finances had deteriorated to this extent, especially considering the monthly payments I had been making in an effort to make amends and tone down some ghosts haunting me. I had hoped that my contribution would ease some of their burden, but clearly, it hadn't been enough.

As we entered the building, the weight of responsibility on my shoulders grew heavier. The realization struck me that the downward spiral had likely started with Anna's death, and the consequences for her family had been far more devastating than I had ever imagined. The guilt gnawed at me, wondering if there was more I could have done if I had only known.

I observed her small frame as she came to a halt in front

of a door covered with graffiti. Her vulnerability and the hardships she endured were etched on her face, and it stirred a determination within me. I was resolved to make things right, to find her brother, and to do everything in my power to rectify the wrongs that had plagued her life.

But as I made this silent promise to myself, doubts crept in. Could I truly save someone when I was haunted by my own ghosts? The shadows of my past lingered, casting doubt upon my ability to provide the redemption she sought.

I owed it to her, to Anna's memory, and my quest for redemption to persevere.

"Honey, is that you?" a woman called as soon as Hope opened the door.

I froze at the woman's voice and threw a questioning look at Hope. I knew that, for some insane reason, Hope didn't blame me for her circumstances, but I knew her parents hated me. Having me there now, with her mother…

Hope's eyes were so sad when she shook her head at me. "Don't worry, she… she is different," she whispered cryptically. "Yes, Mom, it's me," Hope responded, her voice carrying a touch of apprehension.

Her mother's enthusiastic tone hinted at a shift in her demeanor. "Oh, this is wonderful! I'm watching the video of your high school graduation. Come, come, you were so pretty in your dress."

Hope's eyes reflected a profound sadness, silently pleading for my understanding as we stepped farther into the living room. The space was surprisingly cozy and well organized, defying my initial assumptions about the building.

Her mother was sitting on an armchair in a worn-out yellow robe, and a thick blanket rested on her knees. The years had taken their toll on her. It was visible in her gray hair and the lines etched on her face, serving as reminders of the hardships she had endured.

She looked at us and smiled. "Look, Anna sweetheart, wasn't I right to make you choose this blue dress?" she asked Hope.

As I watched Anna's vibrant smile on the screen, my heart ached with the weight of the past and the pain it brought to both Hope and me.

"I know! You're always right, Mom." The sorrow in her voice, the fragility of her smile—it all resonated deeply within me, stirring an impulse I hadn't felt in years.

At that moment, I wanted to be her source of comfort and strength. I wanted nothing more than to wrap my arms around her, hold her tight, and promise her I would do everything in my power to make things right. I wanted to assure her that despite the darkness I carried within me, her life would be different, better, and brighter from that point onward.

Her mother was acting like I was not even there, which was somewhat of a relief because I was uncertain how I would deal with this version of her.

Her mom nodded and turned back toward the TV as if she had now forgotten that Hope was here too.

Hope's fake smile, though strained, remained on her lips as she glanced at me. She was putting up a brave front, concealing her true emotions from her mother. At that moment, I realized the depth of her strength and resilience.

"Come on, let me show you to Leo's room."

As we walked down the corridor, I couldn't help but notice a room with two twin beds. Hope was sharing this room with her mother, and the realization tugged at my heart. The cramped space and lack of privacy spoke volumes about the challenging living conditions they were enduring.

As I stepped into the small room she'd just opened for me, I couldn't help but let out a low whistle. It looked like a hurricane had swept through, leaving belongings scattered and overturned. "Wow, you weren't kidding when you said you already searched his room. You turned it upside down," I commented, hoping to lighten the mood.

She leaned against the threshold and shook her head. "No, it was just like… it was always like that," she said before sighing with resignation.

I wrinkled my nose at the pair of dirty underwear on the side of the room. I might have been obsessively organized, but her brother was a true pig.

"What happened?" I asked as I continued to search the room, my eyes scanning for any possible hiding places or clues that could shed light on her brother's whereabouts.

"About what?" she replied, her voice trembling slightly.

"Your mother," I clarified gently, my gaze focused on the task at hand. I knew it would be easier for her to share if I didn't look directly at her, giving her the space she needed.

"A stroke," she responded, her voice filled with sorrow. "It happened the day before my high school graduation. I think that's why…" Her voice trailed off, leaving the rest of the sentence unspoken.

I glanced her way, and she had difficulty swallowing,

blinking back tears.

The pain I felt on her behalf was almost overwhelming, and I was not certain why it was so intense.

"I think that's why she thought I was Anna. I just… I just didn't want to remind her." As Hope spoke, her voice trembled with emotion, her words punctuated by a heaviness that weighed on her heart.

I nodded, unsure she would have appreciated what I really wanted to say. It was not okay that her mother just erased her from her mind; it was not okay that she pretended to be her dead sister just to keep her mother happy. It was not okay for her brother to be a waste of space, causing her unnecessary worry. Nothing was okay.

Instead, I pushed her brother's bed to reach the vent on the floor. I crouched down and retrieved the small screwdriver from the kit in the side pocket of my leather jacket.

"Are you always traveling with a screwdriver?"

I smiled despite not seeing her; I could imagine the frown of confusion on her delicate brow.

"You know the saying, right? Always be prepared."

"I'm pretty sure it's the Scout motto."

I turned my head to the side and grinned. "Well, Mafia men are Boy Scouts. Everybody knows that."

I felt like a superhero when she let out a little laugh because, despite being short, it was genuine, and I felt damned good for providing her even a few seconds of amusement.

I removed the air vent to find multiple things stacked inside it. *Gotcha!*

"Won't you get into trouble for helping me?" she asked as I was getting everything out.

I kept my back to her to shield her from whatever I would find inside this, but also to keep my emotions in check. I was used to wearing a poker face, hiding my true feelings behind a mask of stoicism and detachment. But Hope, with her presence and her story, had weakened that facade, leaving me exposed and raw.

"What do you mean?" I asked as I went through a stack of poorly taken photos of her brother in various sexual positions with a few men and women.

"You were just passing by, and now you're helping me. Won't Ora be upset?"

"Hoka," I corrected her. I smiled a little as I opened a leather-bound notebook. She was facing all these hardships, worried about her brother, and yet she still worried about me… the man who'd caused her family's downfall. I did not deserve her compassion. "No, he won't be. I—" It was hard to admit it out loud. "I'm not part of the clan anymore."

The silence that descended on the room was suffocating as I flipped through the pages of the notebook, scanning them quickly.

"I'm sorry, Jiro. For whatever happened, I'm sorry."

As I crouched there, my back turned to Hope; I couldn't help but feel overwhelmed by the weight of her undeserved kindness. The genuine concern she showed me, despite knowing the role I played in her family's downfall, was both a testament to her character and a painful reminder of my own mistakes.

Her compassion touched me deeply, and in that moment,

she reminded me a lot of Violet. Both women possessed a strength and resilience that was rare and admirable, and it was no wonder that Hoka had become captivated by Violet. In a world filled with darkness and blood, finding someone like her was a rare and precious gift.

I took a deep breath, steadying myself as I reached the last page of the notebook to find a golden coin taped on it.

As I stared at that golden coin taped to the last page of the notebook, a mixture of anger and disgust surged through me. It was the token given to members of Killian Doyle's sex clubs, a symbol of the illicit activities that took place within those walls. The realization hit me hard—the exorbitant amount of money I had been sending each month to Hope's family had been squandered by her brother for his own perverse pleasures. The monthly fees were exorbitant, but now I was no longer wondering where the ten thousand dollars I sent to her family went. He was using it for his own sexual satisfaction instead of keeping his family healthy and fed. The anger I felt toward Leo intensified. Not only did he add some undue concerns to Hope, but he had also betrayed their trust and used the money meant for their well-being to fuel his own debauchery.

But as my gaze shifted back to Hope, I made a silent vow. I would not let her suffer any longer because of her brother's actions.

I stood up and waved the notebook at her. "I've got everything I need to start. I'll bring you answers soon."

She took a step sideways to stop my exit, a frown on her face. "Where are you going?"

A similar frown of confusion appeared on my face. "To

find your brother?"

She shook her head. "Not without me. I asked for help, not for you to take over."

Oh no, I was not doing that again. The ghosts of what I did to her family haunted me way too much for me just to give in.

"No, absolutely not. You asked me to get involved; it's not for you to get into harm's way. Absolutely fucking not."

"Absolutely *fucking* yes," she replied, and honest to God, she stomped her foot with anger. I had to do my best not to smile at how adorably cute it made her.

I sighed, showing her the coin. "This is a membership to a sex club, Hope, and not the kind you think. It's part of Killian Doyle's Wonderland clubs, a place that caters to those with sexually depraved needs. Is that where you want to go?"

She raised an eyebrow in challenge. "Are you saying that to scare me?"

Yes. "No, I'm just saying this is not a place for a girl like you."

If I thought she was annoyed before, she was furious now. She crossed her arms over her chest and widened her stance, ready for a verbal fight.

"And please do tell, what is a girl like me?"

Beautiful, kind, hopeful, witty, and fierce.

I'd been in a room full of deadly Mafia bosses before, and yet I had never felt as much apprehension as I did now in front of this little but fierce woman.

I sighed instead. "I didn't mean it as an insult, and you know that."

"Tell me, Jiro Saito. Do you know where I work?"

I narrowed my eyes with suspicion at her tone and side smile. I already knew I would hate the answer.

Her smile widened when I remained silent, and she straightened up as if she was about to give me the killing blow.

"I work at *Sex Emporium*."

"Se—What?"

"It's a sex shop in town. One of the most popular, if I may say so myself, so trust me, there's nothing in your little sex club that can shock me."

"*You* work at a sex shop?"

"Uh-huh."

"You? Little Hope Myers."

She stomped her foot again, and I couldn't help but smile this time. She truly was adorable when she was angry. "Stop seeing me as a child! I've grown up, Jiro!"

"Oh, trust me, I noticed!" I snapped back, effectively shutting us both up. I had noticed, of course I had, and it made me feel guilty to have let my eyes linger a little too long on her toned calves, the swell of her breasts, or how perfectly her body molded to mine on the back of the bike.

Yes, I had noticed and enjoyed it all, but Hope may be the only woman I'll never be allowed to touch.

A heavy silence hung in the air after my curt response. The truth of my words lingered between us. I regretted my outburst immediately, knowing that my words had revealed far more than I intended.

Taking a deep breath, I tried to regain my composure. "I'm sorry. That was uncalled for," I said, my voice softer now. "I didn't mean to belittle you or dismiss your maturity. It's just… I have my own mistakes to deal with, and I can't afford for the past to repeat itself. I won't survive it this time."

Hope's expression softened slightly, her anger giving way to understanding and vulnerability. "I know you still feel guilty, but this is a completely different situation." She breathed. "Anna got in the middle of something that had nothing to do with her, something you told her to stay away from."

I frowned at the finality of her voice. "How do you even know that?"

She let out a self-deprecating laugh. "Because I was there. I was everywhere you were. The silly little girl with her stupid crush." Her cheeks turned bright red at the confession. "But that doesn't mean I can't handle my own. It is *my* brother, *my* problem. I asked for your help, not for you to take over, remember?"

I crossed my arms on my chest, not liking that one bit but also knowing that she was right.

She sighed, relaxing her stance. "It's a moot point, anyway. Involve me, don't involve me. I'll keep on looking from my side, and so be it."

I gritted my teeth in frustration at her blatant rejection of her safety. "Fine, but if it gets too dangerous, you're out. No questions asked, deal?"

She raised an eyebrow. "What if I say no?"

I took the few steps separating us and stopped close enough to smell her faint flowery perfume.

"Say no?" I purred with a lower voice.

She looked up, and I couldn't help but grin at her dilated pupils. My presence affected her. Unfortunately, seeing how my body tensed, she affected me just as much.

"Uh-huh."

"Well, sweet Hope, I may have to ground you." My mind went completely blank as I ran my finger slowly along her jawline, making her shiver.

I quickly regained my composure, realizing that I had momentarily allowed my emotions to get the better of me. Taking a step back, I got a hold of myself and cleared my throat.

"Sorry, that was uncalled for," I apologized, feeling a tinge of embarrassment.

Hope nodded, her cheeks slightly flushed. "It's alright," she stated, her voice somewhat breathless. "So, we're good?"

No, we're not. I nodded. "Yes, but we can't just barge into the club, coin or not. It's the best way to get shot. Let me arrange something through Hoka, and we can take it from there. I'll come here tomorrow, and we'll talk."

She shook her head, and I was ready to fight when she extended her hand to me. "I have to do a double shift tomorrow because I ditched today. Let me give you my number."

I gave her my phone and watched as her graceful fingers moved quickly on the screen. "I can come see you at work. Where are you working?"

She frowned, giving me back my phone. "I told you, Sex Emporium."

"You're *not* working in a sex shop."

She glared. "Think what you will, Jiro Saito. It's not like I can argue with you." She pushed from where she stood and gestured to me. "I will see you tomorrow."

I nodded, acknowledging her frustration and the unspoken tension between us. "Okay, see you tomorrow," I replied, trying to keep my tone neutral.

As I turned to leave, I couldn't help but feel a mix of emotions. The unresolved tension between us left a lingering heaviness in the air, and I couldn't shake the feeling that much was left unsaid.

But for now, focusing on finding her brother was the priority.

FOUR

Jiro

Things didn't turn out at all like I had planned. Visiting Anna's grave was supposed to be just a quick stop, a personal introspection, one of the many ghosts I wanted to face and try to exorcise. And then there was Hope... The proverbial hope showed up in the shape of probably the most beautiful girl I had ever seen and the only girl I could never have.

But I could help her, make her life a little better. I had the power to do that, and I wanted to, even if it was the last thing I did.

This was why I was now in a hotel room by the airport instead of being on my way to the next step of my trip.

Where were you going, anyway? The insidious, mocking voice of my conscience asked. I didn't know. I had known nothing except getting on my bike and driving away from Hoka and his new happiness, knowing that my presence would cause him far more trouble than necessary.

I stepped out of the bathroom after my shower and looked at the golden coin that rested beside my phone on the night table.

The internal conflict raged within me as I weighed the options. On the one hand, I could handle the situation on my own, ensuring Hope's safety and sparing her from the dark and dangerous world I suspected her brother was involved in. It would be quicker and more efficient, allowing me to provide her with the answers she sought without putting her at risk.

On the other hand, the thought of her being disappointed, angry, or betrayed by my actions pained me deeply. The idea of leaving her looking at me with any negative emotions was infuriating and unbearable.

I sighed, tightened my wet hair into a bun, and called Hoka.

"Brother, how is the 'introspection tour' treating you?"

I rolled my eyes. "How's fatherhood treating you?"

He sighed in contentment. "Honestly? It's the best thing in the world. I wake up every morning, and I almost can't believe it's all real, and then I go see Yuko and…" He sighed again. "I'm so blessed."

I nodded as guilt crept up again. I almost robbed him of this bliss, all because of my past. I knew he and Violet forgave me despite me being undeserving.

"How is Violet?"

Hoka chuckled. "Violet is a warrior. She is already up and running like she didn't just have a baby. Let me tell you, I will never understand why women are seen as weak. They can take us any day of the week."

I couldn't help but smile, thinking about how Hope stood in my way, ready to fight despite knowing who I used to be.

"I could not agree more."

"What do you need?"

"Why do you say I need something? I may just be calling to check on you."

"You may…" he conceded. "But knowing I saw you less than a week ago, I'm sure there's more."

I sighed, deciding to get straight to the point. "I need to get into one of Doyle's Wonderland clubs."

Hoka whistled between his teeth. "I know you're kinky with the weird piercing you have, but I'm sure you can find whatever you need in any other club. Benetti said something about the Refectory or something in New York."

"I'm still on the West Coast, and I need to get into this one. It's complicated." Boy, was it complicated.

"Which one?"

"Seattle."

"Seattle…" he trailed off, and I knew it would not take him long to make the connection. "Why are you in Seattle, Jiro?"

"Her brother has gone missing." I knew it was better to come clean now; Hoka would know one way or another.

"Jiro." My name in his mouth carried so much weariness and worry that I was not sure I could ease him right now. "How do you even know that?"

I couldn't blame him for being worried about me stepping back into Anna's world again. He'd been so concerned about losing me. The bullets didn't finish the job, but my mind almost did, and it took months to get me out of the depths of depression.

"But this time, it's different. *I'm* different." I took a deep breath, steadying myself as I continued. "Her brother has gone missing, and her sister, Hope, just appeared where I was. It was fate, Hoka, and I know you believe in fate."

There was a moment of silence on the other end, and I could almost feel Hoka processing the information. I knew he would understand. Violet was his destiny; he'd known that from the moment they'd locked eyes.

I sighed. "I couldn't turn her away, not when I saw the pain in her eyes, the weight she carries. I want to find him, to bring him back safe, and to help Hope find the answers she seeks. But I need to enter one of Doyle's Wonderland clubs in Seattle to get the information we need."

Hoka muttered under his breath. "Getting into Doyle's world is difficult, but I'll have a word with Sandro. Maybe he can help."

I pursed my lips. "I'm sure Alessandro Benetti is dying to help me after all the pain I caused his sister."

"You didn't cause his sister pain. *He* did, and you took the fall for him. He owes you that much."

"I didn't do it for him." I was selfless up to a point, and I would never have stepped away from my life, my culture, everything I knew for anyone other than Hoka.

"I know you didn't." Hoka's voice was much softer now. "I'm worried. This place—this family—brings back a lot of dark, scary times. I almost lost you," he admitted, and it was something else that Violet changed in him. He was showing his vulnerabilities now, his doubts, not with everyone, of course, but with the people close to him.

I had difficulty swallowing past the lump of emotions in my throat. There were few people I considered family in this world, and Hoka was it.

"I'm not the same Jiro as I was back then, and I can't walk away just like you would not walk away if Violet had an issue."

"Do you— Was Anna your Violet?"

"Honestly? I don't know." I looked down at the golden token on my night table. "I was… *we were* really young, and she was the first girl I ever loved." *The only girl I ever allowed myself to love.* "And it was almost fleeting. We never got time to come down from the height of passion."

"I see." I didn't miss the cautiousness in his voice.

"What?"

"Nothing."

I sighed. "Hoka, I thought we were past that."

"I just—" He sighed. "I just think that if she had been

your *ikigai*, you would know."

I nodded mutedly. I'd suspected that much once I saw how Hoka loved Violet and how fiercely she loved him back, but it didn't change the fact that her life had been cut short because of me and that an innocent was now six feet under because of my foolishness.

"I need this, Hoka. I need to make amends no matter how foolish it is. I failed you when I didn't support you with Violet. Don't make the same mistake."

He muttered something under his breath and let out a sigh. "Okay, I'll take care of it. Doyle can be…"

"An asshole, yeah."

"Do you need any help?"

I couldn't help the lump of sorrow that formed in my throat. We both knew he couldn't help, not if he didn't want to get himself into more trouble than he already had been. A lesser boss would have been taken down already, with all the exceptions he had made to the Bushido, the ultimate being his marriage to an outsider, and not any outsider, but the sister of an Italian Mafia boss. He had to shun me for the sacrifice I made to ensure his happiness. A sacrifice I owed him after almost destroying his life.

"You know you can't, and I'm okay. It's way beneath my pay grade."

He laughed at my poor attempt at a joke. "Well, the offer stands nonetheless. I'm sure Oda would love to come help, and I'm also almost certain Alessandro would be happy to get rid of him for a while. The kid drives him crazy."

I chuckled. "I'm sure he's doing it because he knows it pisses him off."

Hoka laughed, too. "Yeah, I'm sure of it."

"I'll let you know if I need help, but frankly, I don't think I do. It's so pathetically banal, and it's something we've seen a million times. But I'll let you know if it gets out of hand," I added quickly.

"Okay, and if you want to look into things, all the passwords are the same."

I smiled at that. "Yes, I figured they were. This is my mission tonight." I was planning to look into Hope's life. I saw the sorrow in her face despite how much she was trying to dismiss it, and I wanted to see how deep it ran. I let out a sigh. "You let me know as soon as you hear from Doyle."

"Will do, and you keep in touch, okay?"

"Always. Say hello to Violet for me."

Hoka chuckled. "She's listening. She also worries about you."

That added a fresh coat to the guilt I would probably always carry for the pain I caused her and the loss I couldn't help but feel responsible for. All because I had let my past cloud my judgment.

I opened my mouth to tell them I didn't deserve an ounce of their worry, but they were too stubborn to listen anyway.

"You have a newborn at home. You have better things to do than worry about little old me. Just let me know when Doyle approves, okay? Speak soon."

Before he expressed any further worry, I hung up and settled on the bed with my laptop to dive into the extensive background research and serious invasion of privacy I was about to commit.

I couldn't help but smile a little, imagining how furious Hope would have been if she found out what I was about to do. She was so beautiful when she was angry.

Don't think of her that way. You have no right to do so. You ruined her life.

I spent the next few hours looking into Hope's life for the past few years, and while I had suspected it had been bad despite her dismissal and humbling strength, I had not expected it to be *that* bad.

Her father had died of a heart attack barely a year after Anna's death, and she was left with a grieving, overwhelmed mother and an angry older brother.

I kept on reading despite the growing discomfort. Her mother gave Leo complete control of the finances, and this was when the financial hemorrhage started.

I pursed my lips as my desire to find Anna's brother dimmed as my dislike of him increased with each instance of his frivolous spending. If it were up to me, I'd let him rot in whatever mess he'd put himself in. But there was Hope and how worried she was, how she was looking at me like her knight in shining armor, and I could not let her down. Not again.

I sighed and shook my head, continuing to discover the train wreck her life had been.

She did impressively well at school despite having to work from age sixteen, and then she had to drop out of college despite her stellar grades when her mother got diagnosed with an early onset of Alzheimer's.

I leaned back against my pillow and closed my eyes. How this woman still transpired so much positivity was beyond me. I was completely in awe of her strength. She was much braver than I had ever been.

I groaned, running my hand down my face, knowing that her waste-of-space brother never stepped up, forcing her to do it. The situation was shitty, but he was the oldest. He should have taken care of her, not let her fend for herself and her mother—leaving them barely surviving.

I was going to find the fucker and force him into a room to explain to him what the situation would be like from now on. I had no qualms about threatening and maiming him a little. Hope deserved a better life, and while I could not be the one offering it to her, I could damn well make sure she'd get it one way or another.

I made myself a promise at that moment: I would save her silly brother and save her, too, even if she didn't know she needed saving.

Hope Myers was my mission, my purpose, and my way to atone for my sins, and I would bleed to make it right.

FIVE

Hope

Damn you, Jiro!

"Do you think I'm a prude?" I asked out loud as Max and I worked on the inventory before opening.

"With the way you've been scowling at that nine-inch

alien dildo in your hand for the past five minutes? No, I don't think so."

"I…" I sighed, putting the purple dong on the shelf and grabbing another one from the box. "I'm serious, Max."

He stopped arranging the sensual jewelry from the glass case and turned toward me, his brown eyes full of confusion.

Max was as close to a best friend as one could be, even if this friendship was formed in a very unconventional way. He was my ex-boyfriend's older cousin, and when Jared dumped me for being a *"frigid bitch"* just weeks after I had to drop out of college because my family was broke, Max, against all odds, stood up for me. He offered me a job at his sex shop. It had mortified me at first, but the money was much better than minimum wage, the hours flexible, and the bonus on sales quite enticing. After a while, I started to like it. The customers were far from being the perverts you'd expect; most of them were lovely and fun and even a little shy. The shop was professional and well-organized.

Max was also possibly the nicest man on this earth, always so understanding when I had to bail on short notice, and this is how I was about to celebrate my four-year anniversary at my "temporary" job.

"You're working in a sex shop, for Christ's sake, and I heard you having full-on conversations that would even make *me* blush. No, sweetheart, you're not a prude. You're a gentle, happy soul who's experienced far too much shit in your lifetime."

I nodded, comforted by his pep talk. It was not because I disliked sex that I was a prude. I also disliked being seen as fragile, and somehow, my silly childhood crush on Jiro Saito seemed to still resonate within me, and it really annoyed me to think that he could see any part of me negatively.

"Stupid, tall asshole," I muttered as I grabbed the last sex toy in the box before shoving it on the shelf.

Max closed the case and came toward me, leaning against the shelves beside mine. "Does it have anything to do with the mysterious stranger you ditched me for yesterday?"

I rolled my eyes despite him being spot-on. "It's nothing like that. He—" I stopped talking. I loved Max, and I trusted him, but giving too much information about Jiro could put them both in danger. "I've known him for years, and he's going to find Leo."

Max's taunting smile vanished, replaced with a frown.

I raised a finger in warning. "Don't say it. I know how you feel about all that." I was tired of this discussion.

Max didn't like Leo; he never did and made it abundantly clear, but he had no siblings. He didn't know what it was like, and I assumed losing Anna, his twin, in such a tragic way gave him a little more leeway.

You lost your sister too that day, Max kept repeating when I had to dash. Sometimes, in the middle of my shift, it was to either get my mother from the nearby police station because she left home when he was supposed to look out for her, or I had to go pick him up from some bar because he was much too drunk to drive.

"You matter to me, Hope, you know that."

I nodded. How could I not? He took my side and was far more understanding than was warranted.

I sighed. "I know that. It's just Leo is Leo, and no matter

what…" I shook my head. "I wouldn't even be mad if he just up and left, really, I wouldn't, but I can't just let go with so many uncertainties. I need to know he's okay."

Max raised his hand and brushed my cheek. "I understand, I'm sorry."

I nodded, a little uncomfortable with the contact.

"When we find Leo, I—I think you and I should talk about us. I mean, more where this could be going."

This what? I narrowed my eyes a little. *God, was he blushing?*

I opened my mouth to reply that I was not sure it was the type of discussion I wanted to have with him. My *only* friend… my only constant, but a sharp knock on the door stopped me from answering.

I turned just in time to see Jiro's face as he glared through the window.

I glanced at the clock. "Ah, we're ten minutes late on opening," I started with a sigh of relief to have been spared whatever was about to come out of Max's mouth.

Max snorted as he walked to the door. "Someone has a dildo emergency, it seems."

I couldn't help but chuckle. I could only imagine him saying that to Jiro's face.

As soon as Max unlocked the door, Jiro walked in toward me, completely ignoring him with his trademark scowl on his face.

His aura of authority, danger, and alpha male had me tongue-tied, almost forgetting where I was.

"So, you *do* work here." I narrowed my eyes on him, my previous awe replaced by irritation.

I sighed. "Do you have something new?"

His mouth went up in a small smile. "Is that any way to welcome your friend?"

I felt my cheeks burn with embarrassment but straightened up, not wanting to show him he unsettled me, even if it was probably obvious on my face.

"Are we friends now? I thought you were my knight in shining armor."

His side smile grew as he took another step forward, looming over me, and instead of feeling threatened and overwhelmed, I felt safe.

"Trust me, Hope, I'm no one's savior."

I opened my mouth to contradict him, but Max used this moment to slide between us, facing Jiro and making me take a step back.

"May I help you?" Max asked, crossing his arms on his chest, widening his stance a little.

Even if I only had a view of the back of his neck, I knew that he was scowling—he always had a scowl when he took his "bouncer" pose.

Jiro had a good few inches on Max, even though he wasn't as stocky as Max was. I had felt his hard body yesterday as I rode his bike, and I didn't need to have seen him in action to know that his lean muscles were lethal and that he could probably kill Max in under three seconds.

Jiro looked him up and down, and his previously amused smile turned into a taunting grin.

"I'd advise you to take a step back, Max, my boy," Jiro told him in a low warning tone.

I rolled my eyes and stepped to the side, resting my hand

on Jiro's chest, and immediately regretted my gesture. The heat of his skin under his shirt, the firmness of his pecs… All that was enough to cause a jolt of electricity to go up my arm.

He took a sharp breath, gazing down at me, his pupils dilated, making his dark-brown eyes almost black.

"Max, this is my friend Jiro I told you about." I kept my hand on his chest as I made the introduction while gesturing to Max with my other hand. "Jiro, this is my *boss,* Max." I pressed on the word "boss" to remind him to be civil. I could not say I'd seen Jiro anything but composed, even when he was barely twenty-one, but part of me knew that an angry Jiro would be a force to be reckoned with.

Max turned his scowl toward me. *What did I do now?*

"Boss? This is all I am?" He crossed his arms over his chest.

I winced. He wasn't wrong. "And my friend, of course."

"Friend?" Jiro's smile widened. "How adorable."

I was trying to rack my brain on how to defuse a situation I never thought I would actually face when the bell above the door announced a customer and a blushing girl entered.

I sighed. Throwing my hands up in dismissal to the two men who were a few seconds away from whipping out their dicks in an attempt to assert dominance, I went to the uncomfortable-looking girl who was staring at one of the shelves with fearful, wide eyes.

For the next twenty minutes, I helped her choose her perfect first vibrator while making sure that the two men talking at the back of the store didn't kill each other.

Once she paid, I was about to exit the store when Pedro

walked in with a shit-eating grin on his face.

I threw a quick look to Jiro, who was now focused on me, also very much aware of the change in atmosphere.

I hope he understood what I was not saying. This was the guy that could lead us to Leo.

"Mamacita!" He leaned on the glass counter, peeking behind it. "Wearing a dress? I always love it when you're showing your pretty legs." He jerked his head to the side. "Why don't you come around and give me a hug?"

I forced a laugh despite my discomfort. "I'm working, Pedro."

"*Vale*, what about after work then? I can come pick you up, and we—"

He stopped talking as Jiro approached the counter, standing quite close to Pedro.

"Hope," he said, his voice deeper than I'd ever heard it.

Pedro turned toward him, his flirty look morphing into an annoyed glare. "Why don't you go away, *pendejo*? I'm talking with her. Go look at the cock rings," he added, pointing to the stand against the back wall.

I winced at the rudeness.

Jiro detailed him silently, his gaze taking in every tattoo he could see, including the numbers on the side of Pedro's neck.

Jiro's mouth tipped up at the corner. "Cock rings?" He raised an eyebrow. "I'm sorry, *pendejo,* but I can't wear cock rings—my Jacob's ladder prevents it."

My mouth dropped open at the revelation, my eyes involuntarily jumping to his zipper. He was making that up, wasn't he? Yes, he had to be. Jiro Saito was way too stuck up for anything like that… Or was he?

Didn't they say it was always the quiet ones?

"Eyes up here, sweetheart," Jiro purred.

My gaze flew back to his face, and his previously taunting smile turned into a knowing smirk. What was happening to him? Who was he right now?

"Good girl."

I shivered at the intensity of his eyes, and the heaviness of lust settled in my lower belly, something both unsettling and unfamiliar.

Pedro turned red and started to mutter low threats in Spanish toward Jiro, who turned back toward him. His previously playful look transformed into smooth impassiveness, which I suspected was way worse than anger.

"You know, my man, sometimes you should be careful who you're talking to." Jiro turned toward me. "But even if cock rings are out of the question, maybe you can recommend new nipple rings," he added, lifting his T-shirt, revealing a tattoo-covered chest so perfect it seemed to have been carved in marble and painted by Leonardo da Vinci himself.

My jaw went slack at the view and at the small hoop he had on each nipple before my eyes dipped down once again to his zipper, wondering if his previous statement had been the truth.

Unfortunately, it was something I would never know.

Pedro's reaction was completely different but just as intense as mine as he kept his eyes on Jiro's rib cage, his face as pale as a ghost.

"I—I didn't know." He took a step back, raising his hands in surrender. "I didn't know," he repeated.

I frowned, concentrating on the same area Pedro had been looking at, but I didn't see what scared him so much. It was just a snake intertwined... with the number *893*.

The dim light seemed to play on Jiro's skin as he pulled down his shirt, the fabric hiding a canvas of well-chiseled muscle that I had only just been privy to. I took a moment, letting my eyes wander over him before turning my attention to Pedro, who had edged farther toward the door, a clear wariness in his eyes.

"She never mentioned being taken," Pedro stammered, his hands raised in a gesture of placation.

I could only shake my head in disbelief. Such a cowardly move to shift the blame.

Jiro's voice cut through the room, deep and smooth, "Well, she is."

A gasp escaped my lips when I felt his hand delicately touch the nape of my neck, a gentle pressure that sent electric jolts straight to my core. My pulse raced as his fingers brushed my skin, and I leaned into his touch, drawn to him like a magnet.

When he tilted my face toward his, his voice dropped an octave, tinged with a huskiness that made my heart race. "Now you know."

His gaze lingered on my lips, filled with a hunger and passion that left me breathless. And then, without warning, he closed the distance between us. His lips met mine in a storm of raw desire, taking me by surprise and pulling me into a whirlwind of sensations. The world dissolved around me, and all I could feel was the heat of his kiss and the yearning building within.

My fingers found their way to the hem of his T-shirt, clutching it tight, trying to bring him impossibly closer. The intoxicating blend of his scent—musk and something uniquely Jiro—consumed me. Each touch, each caress, only deepened the passion and made me lose myself more in the moment.

The world came crashing back when our lips parted. In the aftermath of our heated exchange, I realized Pedro had vanished, and Max's disapproving eyes bore into us.

Blinking a few times, I tried to gather my thoughts, but my emotions were in turmoil. Jiro, however, looked unflustered, his fingers deftly working his phone as if our fervent kiss was but a fleeting distraction.

He glanced up briefly, his voice cool and detached. "Pedro won't be troubling you again. You're welcome."

His nonchalance felt like a cold splash of water. The raw intimacy we had just shared reduced to a mere transaction. I was a damsel he had saved, nothing more. The realization stung, reminding me that in Jiro's mind, I was just another problem for him to solve, another complication in his already complicated life.

As much as I tried to deny it, I couldn't ignore the truth. I was not relevant to Jiro Saito. Our brief connection meant nothing to him in the grand scheme of things. I was just a girl caught up in his world of darkness and danger.

I took a deep breath, trying to compose myself and push down the hurt I felt. "Thank you," I replied, my voice steady despite the turmoil inside. "For taking care of Pedro and for helping me with my brother. I appreciate it."

Jiro glanced at me, and for a moment, I saw a flicker of something in his eyes—regret, maybe? But it was gone as quickly as it came, and his expression became unreadable again.

"You don't have to thank me," he said, his tone distant. "It's what I do."

I nodded, understanding that this was who he was, the person he had become: Jiro Saito, the man who navigated the shadows and dealt with darkness. And I was just a girl who happened to cross his path.

Jiro's phone vibrated in his hand, and I could sense his growing frustration. As he glanced at Max, I could see the tension between them, even if I didn't really understand the reason behind it.

"I have a few things to take care of," Jiro muttered, his jaw ticcing with annoyance. He then turned his attention back to me. "When are you finishing?"

"Six."

He nodded. "I'll meet you back here at six."

Before I could agree, Jiro turned to Max and spoke in a low, commanding voice. "You make sure she's safe, yes? It shouldn't have been that hard to get that creep away."

Max's scowl deepened. "Pedro was not a threat. You're just exaggerating. I'm Hope's friend, and before yesterday, I never even heard your name, so no offense, *pal*," he spat the word with derision, "I know how to take care of her."

Jiro scoffed. "How nice it must be to be so delusional." He waved toward me. "I'll see you later," he added before turning around and leaving the store stiffly.

The rest of my shift was the worst I had ever experienced, with Max being in the darkest mood I'd ever seen him, muttering to himself and leaving me alone and bored behind the counter.

I was relieved when the clock hit six and quickly said goodbye to a still-sulking Max and exited the store as dusk fell.

Jiro was already there, leaning against his bike, his expression unreadable.

As I approached, he straightened up, his intense gaze fixed on me.

"What was that all about?" I asked as I reached him on the sidewalk.

He extended me his spare helmet. "I'm hungry."

"I'm serious," I insisted, crossing my arms on my chest.

"So am I!" He nudged the helmet toward me again, and I grabbed it automatically. "I saw a Mexican truck by the pier. Let's eat and talk."

My stomach squeezed, reminding me that food seemed to be a good idea right about now, so I pushed the helmet on my head. "Mexican sounds good."

A small smile tugged at the corner of his lips. "Thought so." He turned toward the bike and straddled it. "Come on, let's go."

I couldn't help the little jitter of excitement as I sat behind him… pressing my body against his, wrapping my arms around his hard chest. Was it something you ever got used to? I didn't think so, not with Jiro.

As we rode through the city, the exhilaration of the bike ride, mixed with the closeness of our bodies, made my heart race. I could feel the warmth of Jiro's back against my front, his muscles tensing as he navigated through the streets. It was an intoxicating sensation, and I relished every moment.

The closer we got to the pier, the stronger the sea smell, and while I was happy to finally get some answers, I was also a little disappointed to let go of my hold on him.

As he parked by the truck, I was pleased to see that only a couple of tables were taken, allowing us to have a more private conversation.

"What do you want?" he asked after securing the helmets on the bike.

"Fish tacos."

He raised an eyebrow. "Fish from a van?" He grimaced. "I commend you."

I shrugged. "I like to live on the edge."

His expression turned from teasing to serious in a second. "Don't I know it." He looked up and sighed. "Grab a table. I'll be right there."

I grabbed a table farthest from the food van and sat down, watching as Jiro approached the vendor to order our tacos.

As I waited for him to return with the food, I couldn't help but reflect on how his simple presence changed everything. There was a sense of comfort in his presence, even amid all the chaos and uncertainty.

He returned with a tray of fish tacos, and I couldn't help but smile at the sight. It was a simple gesture, but it meant so much to me. "Fish too, huh?"

He shrugged. "Ah, well, if you die, I'll die too," he said before taking a bite.

This slipup drained all humor from the moment, and both of us turned serious at once.

"How was your shift?"

"Long." I rested my fingers on my lips, replaying the kiss.

Jiro's eyes trailed to my lips, darkening. "The asshole will not bother you anymore."

I nodded, looking down at the taco on my plate. Of course, there was no other motive.

"Was your boyfriend pissed?"

"He's my friend."

Jiro shook his head with a snort. "Does he know that?"

I frowned, finally catching up on what he'd said before when he came earlier today, and I froze as things clicked into place.

"How did you know his name?"

His back straightened as he looked up slowly. "What?"

"Max, how did you know his name?"

"You introduced us."

I shook my head. "No, you knew before."

He threw me a wary look.

I sighed, feeling the weight of the unspoken truth between us. "Jiro, please don't lie to me. I know you knew Max's name before I introduced you. How?"

He hesitated for a moment as if debating whether or not to tell me the truth. Finally, he let out a sigh and looked away. "Okay, fine. I knew his name because… because I've been looking into your life and, as I expected, things have been a lot tougher for you than you told me."

I shrugged. "I guess we're both hiding things."

"We are…" he admitted with another sigh.

"What is it you showed Pedro that scared him that much?"

He looked up from his plate, detailing my face as he chewed on his taco. "I showed him who I was," he replied evasively.

I shook my head with frustration; this was bound to become tiring soon.

He sighed. "You said it yourself. When you met me, I had fewer tattoos. Most of what I have has nothing to do with aesthetics. They are…" He cocked his head to the side. "Codes, if you will, of what I've done, who I am, and who I belong to."

"You're still with the—" I looked around before leaning over the table. "*Them*," I whispered urgently.

Jiro leaned forward as well, a soft smile on his lips. "Technically, I'll always be." He detailed my face for a second before leaning back on his seat, creating a distance that annoyed me. He waved his hand dismissively. "These codes are widely known within other organizations."

Organizations… a civilized word for gangs.

Jiro's eyes glinted with this savage light I'd seen a couple of times before. "He obviously could read the signs well enough."

"Will you tell me?"

"Not today, Hope, not today," he let out a little wistfully before looking at his watch. "Come on, let's finish our dinner. I am waiting for Hoka to call me when he's back from his trip. It may be a few days, but I promise I'll come find you as soon as I have news."

I didn't know why, but this was just his version of running away to keep his walls up, and instead of pressing, I let it go because despite what I wanted to believe, Jiro was not mine—he was not mine when I was a silly enamored child, and he was not mine now. He was a temporary feature, and I could not let myself see what was under his armor because I feared what I would discover may not make me run away but fall deeper.

Six

Jiro

Temporary insanity.

It had to be that. I didn't know why I kissed her. I certainly didn't need to show him the side of my chest, which showed both my allegiance to the yakuza and my initial status of executioner. He'd been scared enough, but I'd been in a dark mood when I'd shown up at the store, seeing that stupid Max standing much too close to her, *touching* her like he was entitled to.

Maybe he was entitled to, certainly more than I was, and yet it'd unsettled me in the most unreasonable way possible.

I thought back to all the times Hoka had taken what I considered stupid and reckless decisions as far as Violet was concerned, and I suddenly didn't feel like pointing my finger at him anymore.

Everything I'd done with Hope so far was out of character—the jealousy, the sense of ownership I was unfamiliar with... the sense of belonging. So, I did what I always did best when my feelings were involved. I fled. Well, metaphorically, at least, because while she's not seen me for the past three days, I've seen her, following her around town like her shadow as she was oblivious to my presence. I was too scared to slip again, knowing that this time I may not stop taking what my irrational mind kept screaming was mine.

My heart fluttered as she exited the sex shop to rush into the coffee shop just beside it, dressed in an adorable white dress with cherries on it and matching red Converse.

Koi no yokan, my mind whispered, and I hated that. The ancestors couldn't be that cruel, could they? They could not give me a soul mate who was so forbidden—the little sister of the woman I killed. I was the source of this family's misery.

I snorted. Of course, they would! Sadistic bastards. What better way to make me pay for my sin than to give me something I could never keep?

My phone vibrated in my pocket, and I took a few steps back into the side alley across the road from her store, hiding myself from any potential sighting.

I let out a huff of relief at seeing Hoka's name on the screen. The sooner we fixed the problem, the sooner I could leave and forget Hope.

Will you?

"Hey! I've good news… under conditions," Hoka announced as soon as I answered.

I was grateful for his direct nature. I didn't have time for mindless chitchat right now.

I snorted. "Of course there is. It's Doyle, after all."

"You're good to go on Saturday, but you have to bring the girl. He's under the assumption you would do nothing reckless with her as potential collateral damage."

I pursed my lips. He was right… clever bastard.

I'd planned to do that part of the mission without her, no matter what I had promised or how angry she might have been. I was sure she wouldn't be mad once I dropped her useless brother in front of her door.

"Okay, that's it?"

"Not quite." Hoka let out a huff of irritation. "You can only ask questions about her brother or his associate. Anyone else is off-limits."

I scoffed, shaking my head. "Like I care about his list of perverts."

"And you can't use any room or any girl."

"Obviously!" None of the girls appealed to me, but the rooms… that was a whole different story. I couldn't help but imagine Hope with me in one of them for a second.

I hissed as I felt my hardening length press against the front of my zipper and switched my stance to ease my discomfort. "What was it like not to have control of your head and cock once you met Violet? Did you ever consider throwing yourself off a fucking bridge?" I blurted out, not having only lost control of my body and lust but my mind too.

The line was eerily silent for a second, and I even stopped breathing. Apparently, the insanity went much further than I initially expected to make me voice this out loud.

"Jir—"

"I also may need Oda after all," I added quickly, knowing there was no way he didn't hear what I just said, but also determined to pretend it didn't happen.

"Jiro." I hated the worry that my name alone carried.

"I knew the brother was involved with local gangs," I continued as if he had not spoken at all. "But I think it's not just any stupid gang. One of them came to Hope's store, and based on his tattoos, he's a soldier of the Valdez cartel."

"Oh." That stirred Hoka's mind right out of my stupid admission. "We don't have bad blood with Valdez—I'll go even as far as to say they owe us one for not meddling when the Chinese asked."

I twisted my mouth to the side. That was true. "I suppose so, but I'm not a yakuza anymore. I have no weight to talk to Valdez."

"You'll always be a yakuza, Jiro."

"I know, but if things went south…" I trailed off. I didn't need to add what we both knew. I would not have any legitimacy to ask for backup.

"I'm sure this can be arranged," he added.

I pursed my lips. Having Oda here was an added complication as a hint of jealousy started to spread into my mind.

Oda was all my good things and none of my bad. He was young and not yet broken. He was annoyingly funny and strong—someone who would be perfect for Hope if she was so adamant about sinking into this type of darkness, and yet I couldn't accept that.

"How is she doing? Hope, is that right?"

I couldn't help but smile at Hoka's not-so-discreet way of fishing for information, and I could not blame him after the teenage boy hormonal outbreak he'd just witnessed.

"Yes, it's Hope, and you know it." I sighed. "She's something else, you know? And I don't think she sees it herself. She went through a *staggering* amount of shit, and she's still so brave, forgiving, and radiating goodness. It's humbling, really."

"Yes, they have to be particularly strong to be *ikigai* for men like us. It takes an impressive amount of strength, both mental and emotional, to be the soul mate of a yakuza."

I leaned my back against the brick wall, resting my hand over my heart and the painful echo his words caused.

"She is *not*. She *can't* be."

Hoka sighed. "Maybe, maybe not, but I know from experience that even if it is rarely convenient, it's worth it."

"I—" How could I build a future on the ghosts of my past? "Let me know when Oda is on the way, okay?"

Hoka sighed again. I swear that had become his

automatic response to me these days. "And you'll let me know what you find out, okay? Yakuza or not, you're my brother. I have your back."

I nodded, even if he couldn't see me, knowing full well that if things really went south, I would never involve him. He was the head of the yakuza, yes, but he was also a loving husband and doting father. I destroyed a family once and almost destroyed Hoka's shot to a happy ending. I would not do it again.

"I'll keep you posted." I put the phone back in my pocket, and as soon as I walked out of the alley, I met the blue eyes of a furious Hope.

She was standing a few steps away, her arms crossed over her chest, one Converse-clad foot tapping on the sidewalk, and with her adorable angry frown on her face.

Why did angry Hope elate me? Why was her anger pleasing me? Because I was a sick fuck!

"Why are you following me?"

"Who says I'm following you?" I asked, closing the distance between us and standing close enough for her to kick.

Her frown deepened, and her eyes flickered to my crotch. I had to stop my smile from spreading, knowing she probably pictured kicking me in the balls.

I took a step back just in case. That kitten had claws.

"I'm not an idiot, Jiro! And you could come and talk to me like a normal person instead of following me in the shadows. Plus, you shouldn't do that. You're terrible at it."

I raised my eyebrows. No, I wasn't terrible at it. I was excellent at it—even better than trained spies. I was a *kage* yakuza… a shadow before rising to Hoka's right hand.

"Is that right?"

She huffed and nodded. "Yes, I knew you were there the whole time."

I cocked my head to the side. "You saw me?" I doubted it.

She twisted her mouth, fidgeting on her feet. "No, I just knew."

That was devastating news because it confirmed what I feared. She could feel me just as I felt her. She was my goddamned *ikigai*. Fuck!

"Jiro?" Her anger morphed into concern, and I was wondering how much of my desperation she could see.

I forced a smile, pointing at the store. "Won't you be in trouble with the boss man if you stay too long?"

She glanced toward the store before looking back at me. "No, I was not supposed to work today. Just catching some hours, and I have something planned for the afternoon."

Both my curiosity and jealousy were piqued. "Is that right? Can I join you? It would be easier than, you know… following you like a creep."

She tried to glare, but a lovely pink hue of self-consciousness covered her cheeks and neck. "I… You know it's not interesting. I'm spending the afternoon at Belleview Center."

"That's where your mother goes, isn't it?"

She nodded. "Yes, three days a week, and in exchange for the preferential rate, you can offer your time. So they have me one afternoon per week."

My annoyance and dislike for her brother came back

like a tidal wave. With the money I had been sending, she could have easily finished her schooling and got her mother to that center full time without the need to trade her time for a meager three days.

I opened my mouth, wanting to tell her how much of a waste of space her brother truly was and that maybe she shouldn't waste too much of her worries on him. Maybe she should just leave him where he was—dead or alive—and take back control of her life. I'd give her all the money she wanted. She was only twenty-two; she could go back to school, set her mother in full-time care, and live. It was not too late for her.

It is not too late for you… The insidious voice in the depths of my chest piped in, allowing me to wonder how I could fit into her narrative. Could I make it? Be the doting househusband living in our little house in a suburb—with our white picket fence, our Sunday barbecues, and our—

"Jiro?"

I blinked as she waved her hand in front of my face.

A profound sense of mortification swallowed me, and it was not a feeling I was used to or had ever really experienced.

"Yes, I was just thinking. I'm sure they could use another pair of hands, right?"

She shrugged. "Well, of course, they always can. They are overworked and underfunded, but…" She looked up at me, twisting her plump mouth to the side. "I don't think it's for you, Jiro, it's…" She shook her head with a little grimace.

Her half-spoken thoughts grated me the wrong way and

also hurt me a little. I knew who I was; I never made a secret of it, and in the grand scheme of things, she was right. I was, and have been, an executioner for the yakuza, but I was so much more, and I wanted her to see that.

It was irrational. Of course it was. I had claimed to want to keep the distance, that I was all wrong for her, and yet I wanted her to see me under all the right lights.

I wanted her to see the potential, no matter how stupid it was.

"You don't think I'm able to help someone other than with my katana and guns? I'm more than just death and destruction, you know." I meant to say it in a joking tone, but it came out far more intense than I intended.

She widened her eyes. "No!" she gasped, resting her hand on my chest.

I was not sure of the reason. Maybe it was to reassure me, or perhaps she was acting on a pull we probably both felt, but feeling her touch me burned my skin deliciously, even through my shirt.

She took a sharp breath, and as she tried to remove her hand, my instincts took over and pressed mine on top of hers, stopping her retreat. I liked the contact. I was not ready for it to stop.

"Let me come, please. Let me show you I'm far more than you think."

She kept her eyes on my hand on top of hers. Her pupils dilated, and goose bumps spread on her arm as I ran my thumb back and forth on the back of her hand.

"I—yes, of course." She stopped looking at our hands and looked up at my face, the apple of her cheeks still pink.

"I just didn't want you to get bored. It's nothing glamorous."

"No?" I raised an eyebrow. "And here I thought that care homes were the underground Mafia of Seattle."

Her shoulders relaxed as she let out a little laugh. "You'd be surprised. Okay, fine. You're welcome to join."

And then, I was not really sure why I did what I did. I grabbed her hand from my chest and kissed her palm before letting it go.

"Oh!" Her face turned beet red, and I quickly turned around, hoping she didn't see how much it had unsettled me, too.

A chaste brush of my lips on her palm affected my body in ways that even the most depraved sex never did. I turned my head to the side, finding her still cradling her hand. "Come on, Hope Myers, let's go."

I didn't know what the future held; I didn't even know what Hope and I were going to become or not, but I knew one thing for sure.

I would not be the same man when I left as I was when I came.

SEVEN

Hope

"Seventy-four, under the O, seventy-four!" I called before putting the bingo ball in the yellow bucket by my side.

"Seventy-four hit the floor!"

"That's right." I laughed, turning toward Mrs. Wallace,

who was sitting at the table near the front, which was the same table as my mother and Jiro.

My heart squeezed in my chest at seeing him hunched over his own bingo card, glancing at my mom's card, too, making sure she was not missing a number. He had his eyebrows furrowed, taking this far more seriously than winning a crochet set warranted.

I smiled with a little shake of my head as I turned the wheel again before picking another ball.

"Ten, under the *B*, ten!"

"Bingo!" an older man at the back called, followed by a very vocal "motherfucker" coming from Jiro.

My mother cracked a smile at his expletive; it was one of her good days.

"Okay, let's take a short break while I check the ticket, and next up will be a spa basket. See you all back in fifteen minutes."

I went off the stage with my list of numbers and checked the older gentleman's card as the gentle buzz of conversation settled on the room.

Once I checked the numbers and congratulated the winner, I approached the table where Jiro and my mother were seated to get them some drinks.

"We'll get that damned spa set, Liliane. God be my witness," he said, leaning toward my mother.

My heart leaped in my chest as she reached for him and patted his cheek. "It's okay. It's fun."

How was it possible for me not to fall for him?

"You're a good man. I'm happy Hope has you. She deserves to be happy, you know that, little one."

I rested my hand on my mouth to muffle my gasp of surprise. It was so rare that she remembered me.

Jiro grabbed her hand and kissed the back of it. "I will take care of our Hope, Liliane. This is my vow to you."

My mother nodded and looked behind her, smiling when she saw me. "Oh, Anna! I'm thirsty. Could you get me a lemonade, please, sweetheart?"

My smile wobbled as I deflated. I had hoped just for a few seconds that maybe she would call me by my name.

I nodded. "Of course, Mom. Do you want anything?" I asked, concentrating on Jiro. The intensity of his eyes on me made me shiver.

"No, I'm fine."

I nodded again and brought her the drink before going back to the bingo game, somehow feeling a little heavier than I was at the start. Hearing her mentioning "Hope" and still calling me "Anna" really dampened my mood for the rest of the bingo event.

"Are you okay?" Jiro asked, coming to stand beside me as I looked at the center's staff herding the patients back inside for the rest of the day's activity.

I started to nod but stopped myself. I didn't feel like faking it anymore today, and not with Jiro. "It's just hard to get reminded of the fucked-up reality, even if it's daily."

He took a side step closer to me and wrapped his arm around my shoulders, pulling me to his chest.

I grabbed his shoulders, rejoicing in the comfort of his body heat, his firm muscles, and the faint smell of his cologne.

"Facing the truth is hard, but it's often for the best. It's when we delude ourselves that we cause pain around us."

I pulled my head back but kept my grip on him. Not ready to break the contact yet.

"Truth…" I trailed off. Maybe it was time for me to face the truth, too. "He's dead, isn't he? Leo," I said, barely louder than a whisper.

Jiro sighed, pulling me closer before looking around the empty room. "It's possible but unlikely." He shook his head. "Your—" He stopped talking and looked around the room again.

"You're just as safe to talk here than anywhere else. Nobody cares about this place."

He looked thoughtful for a few seconds, then nodded. "Your brother is involved with the Valdez cartel." He continued, his voice significantly lower than before. "Valdez is a sick motherfucker, and he loves to make his kills a cautionary tale for everyone. I would have expected his body to have come back up by now."

"So it's a good thing, right?"

He let go of me, and I reluctantly let go as well.

He grimaced, leaning back against the table. "In a sense that he's still breathing—yes, I guess so, but that doesn't automatically mean he's okay." He shrugged. "Best-case scenario, he just up and became a full-time thug."

I frowned, somehow disliking the thought of my brother putting us, putting me, in this type of mental torture. But maybe he would. I snorted. Yeah, come to think of it, he totally could.

Jiro detailed me, his head cocked to the side. "It stung to think about it, right?"

I shook my head a little.

Jiro waved his hand in a dismissive gesture. "He could also be held against his will because he knows or has something Valdez wants, or he's been sent for a mission somewhere."

"I just want an answer… whatever it is."

He nodded, looking away thoughtfully.

"I looked into that club, the one with the coin," I admitted. I wanted to give him back the sincerity he'd just given me.

He turned back toward me, a disapproving scowl etched between his eyebrows.

"I didn't do anything dangerous," I quickly added, raising my hands in surrender. "Some of the girls working there come into the emporium, and I just, you know…" I shrugged. "I think it's a wrong lead."

"Okay…" he trailed off, burying his hands in his pockets. "Why do you think that?"

"Not that I think Leo is a saint or anything, but the girls said it's super expensive and very exclusive. We don't have any powerful friends, and we sure as hell don't have the money." I snorted; we were poor nobodies.

Jiro's eyes flashed with a sort of indignation I could not really place before he moved from his spot on the table. "Do we need to take your mother home?"

I narrowed my eyes at the abrupt change of subject. "No, they will bring her back with the van later."

He jerked his head toward the door. "Okay, let's go then."

"No, no." I stayed where I stood. "I thought we were

doing things with complete honesty now. What was that look about?"

"You had that money."

I laughed. "I can assure you we did not."

He sighed, looking heavenward. "Listen, it's not great to talk about people who—"

I stomped my foot. "Talk, Jiro."

He looked down at my Converse, a slight smile on his face. He seemed to like me best when I was frustrated with him.

"I've been sending you money for quite some time."

I took a step back with shock and also a hint of embarrassment at his pity. "How long?"

"Listen, Hope, it doesn't rea—"

I stomp my foot again. "HOW. LONG?"

"Probably since the start."

"Oh…" I sat heavily on a chair that was still pulled back, grateful we stayed in the room after all. I could hardly believe the hypocrisy of my parents and brother. During all these years, they cursed Jiro while taking his money. "How much?"

"It doesn't matter."

"Jiro, how much?"

"Enough to pay for the club," he replied evasively, and I was too shaken by the revelations and all that it implied.

I had lost the will to fight as tears of defeat started to prickle at the back of my eyes. I thought we'd just got bad luck and that we all suffered, but it seemed that I was the one who got the brunt of it. If Jiro had sent us enough money to cover the astronomical fees this club was costing, I could have easily finished college and probably…

"Don't go there."

I looked up at Jiro through the light haze of unshed tears as he now stood in front of me.

"What?" My voice cracked at the word.

He muttered something in Japanese before crouching in front of me. "This is why I didn't want to tell you, at least not yet. There's no point dwelling on things you may never get answers to. There's no point getting lost in the 'what could have been.'"

He grabbed my hands in his, and I looked down as they rested on my lap. His strong hands engulfed mine, warming my freezing fingers.

I looked back at him silently; his face was so close, his eyebrows slightly etched as his eyes scanned my face with concern.

"These thoughts arc poisonous, Hope. Take it from someone who knows. Nothing, and I mean *nothing*, good can come out from the path your thoughts were taking." He tightened his hold on my hands, bringing one to his mouth and kissing the back of it.

It was an innocent gesture, a gentle attempt to comfort me, and yet the simple brush of his lips seemed to wake all my nerves, turning my blood into liquid fire. How was that possible?

"Is that why you came?" I asked him, this question still occupying the forefront of the mystery that Jiro Saito was.

He stayed crouched in front of me as his thumb brushed back and forth on my knuckles.

"No, I came to find a way to let go of it, actually. I didn't leave the clan, Hope. I was cast away." He looked away sharply, and I pursed my lips, stopping myself from saying anything—breaking the confession I assumed was hard for him to make.

He took a deep breath. "I deserved it, I did, and even if I'm gone, Hoka is still my brother. But I've let my past… my *own* interpretation of it impact the future of people I love, and I can't do that anymore, and I can't allow you to take this path either." He let go of my hand and cupped my cheek.

I closed my eyes, nuzzling shamelessly in the kind, gentle gesture.

"Hope, whatever happened, happened. There is no benefit of you mulling over how things could have been or how they should have been. You're twenty-two, you've got your whole life in front of you. Let's concentrate on that."

I closed my eyes, turned my head into his hand, and kissed his palm. He took a sharp intake of breath, and I opened my eyes, surprised to find him so close, his nose almost touching mine.

"You're right. It's not too late to go for what I want." My heart pounded in my chest, and in a moment of bravery or complete insanity, I leaned forward and pressed my lips against his. His hand on my cheek tensed, pulling me closer, and I responded with a soft sigh, deepening the kiss. The taste of him was intoxicating, a blend of danger and desire that I couldn't resist. His hand still cupped my cheek, his thumb brushing against my skin, sending shivers down my spine. The intensity of his touch, the way his lips moved against mine, ignited a fire within me that I had never felt before.

The sound of a loud crash from the corridor snapped us back to the present, and Jiro abruptly pulled away.

He stood up briskly and stepped back, his hand running through his hair in a gesture of frustration. "Hope, I…" His words faltered, a heavy sigh escaping his lips. Regret shadowed his features, his eyes avoiding mine.

My heart sank, the warmth of the moment replaced by a cold wave of disappointment. I had let myself believe, even for a brief moment, that he felt the same way I did. But now, his sudden withdrawal told me a different story.

"It's okay," I said softly, though the ache in my chest told me it was anything but okay. I wrapped my arms around myself as if that could protect me from the sudden chill that had settled over us.

Jiro looked at me, his gaze haunted by a storm of conflicting emotions. "Hope, I didn't mean… I shouldn't have…"

"It's fine," I repeated, my voice a mere whisper. I fought to keep the hurt from showing in my eyes, to keep the sting of tears at bay. I had known the risks, after all. Jiro was a tortured man haunted by his past. By my sister's ghost, and I had no right to expect anything more from him.

His jaw tightened, a muscle twitching as he clenched it. "Let me take you home," he said, his voice strained.

I stood up from my chair and nodded, unable to trust my voice. We walked to his bike in silence, the weight of unspoken words heavy between us. As we rode, the wind whipped through my hair, and I held on tightly, trying to focus on the rush of adrenaline rather than the ache in my chest.

The ride back to my apartment felt like an eternity, each passing second amplifying the emptiness I felt. When we finally arrived, I quickly dismounted the bike, my movements almost frantic. I didn't want him to see the tears that threatened to spill over.

"Thanks for the ride," I said, happy that my voice sounded clear as I extended the helmet back to him. "I'll see you on Saturday for the club."

I turned away from him, fumbling for my keys and practically sprinting up the path to my building.

"Hope," his voice called after me, tinged with an urgency that only added to the turmoil inside me.

I didn't turn back. I couldn't. I unlocked the door and rushed inside, my heartache a heavy weight on my chest.

I ran up the stairs to my apartment, and once I was securely inside, I leaned against the closed door, letting out a shaky breath.

Tears blurred my vision, and I angrily brushed them away. I had known anything between us was impossible, but knowing didn't make it hurt any less. I had opened my heart, letting myself hope for something more, and now I was left with the bitter taste of rejection.

I walked into our sparse living room and slouched onto our ratty couch. I let the tears finally fall, allowing myself a moment of vulnerability in the privacy of my own home. Jiro's face flashed in my mind, his touch still lingering on my skin, and I pushed away the ache, the disappointment.

I had faced worse challenges in my life, and I wasn't about to let a moment of heartache define me. With a determined sigh, I wiped away the tears, stood up, and set my focus on the future. Whatever it held, I would face it with strength and resilience, just as I always had.

EIGHT

Jiro

I stood outside Doyle's club, my irritation simmering just beneath the surface as I checked my watch again.

Hope had insisted on taking a taxi, refusing my offer to pick her up. Stubborn, as always. But I couldn't help the frustration that gnawed at me. It was ridiculous, really, to be annoyed about something so trivial. But it was more than that. It was the constant reminder that I had no right to be here, no right to claim any part of her life. And also a reminder that, despite all that, I hated when she put any kind of distance between us. No matter how justified it was.

And then the taxi pulled up, and my breath caught in my throat. Hope stepped out, a vision of beauty that left me momentarily speechless. Her short black dress clung to her body in all the right places, showing well-toned legs under fishnet tights. Her lavender hair fell in waves around her shoulders. She was undeniably desirable, a fact that hit me like a punch to the gut, especially knowing the lustful looks she would get once we stepped into this den of sex.

She approached with that cool indifference in her eyes, a shield that she seemed to have built against me. It was a stark contrast to the warmth and openness I had seen in her before. I couldn't help but feel a pang of frustration at the distance she was putting between us.

I had taken extra care with my appearance tonight, hoping to erase some of the damage my unwilling rejection caused. My clothes were impeccable, and my hair meticulously styled. But it seemed to be in vain. Her cool gaze skimmed over me as if I were just another stranger.

"Hey," she greeted, her voice polite but distant. Her eyes met mine, a cautiousness lurking in their depths that I hadn't seen before. It was as if she had built a protective shield around herself, one I wasn't sure I could breach.

"Hey," I replied, my voice rougher than I intended. I wanted to reach out, to pull her close and forget about everything else. But the memories of my past mistakes held me back, a reminder that I didn't deserve her.

I cleared my throat, trying to steer the conversation to safer waters. "How have you been?" I asked. A simple question that held more weight than I could express.

"I'm sorry for being late. The friend who usually takes care of my mother was delayed at work," she replied, ignoring my question.

Had she been just as miserable as I had?

My attention drifted, and I noticed the way some men were eyeing her. A surge of jealousy shot through me, an irrational possessiveness that clashed with my sense of responsibility. I wanted to reach out, to bridge the distance between us, but I held back. The ghosts of my past whispered in my ear, a constant reminder that I was no good for her, that I could only bring her pain. I had no right to feel this way, not after what I had done.

"Are you alright?" Her voice cut through my thoughts, her eyes searching mine for answers.

"Yeah, I'm okay," I replied, offering a small smile. "Just lost in thought."

She seemed to study me for a moment as if trying to decipher the turmoil in my gaze. The questions were there in her eyes, but I couldn't bring myself to answer them.

She sighed. "Shouldn't we go in? I'm not comfortable being outside like this."

I looked at her suggestive dress, leaving little to the imagination, and sighed. It was going to be a very long evening.

"Okay, let's go." I rested my hand against her soft, bare

back and cursed the situation even more.

What would have happened if things were different? I shook my head just as we reached the security at the entrance of the club.

I was doing *exactly* what I told her not to do. I was getting lost in what could have been.

"Name?" the man said, his eyes narrowing on the tattoo peeking out at the side of my neck. He moved a little, causing his jacket to open slightly and reveal his gun.

I had to admit I admired his smoothness and not-so-subtle warning.

"Jiro Saito."

The man scanned his clipboard. "You're not on the list."

"The other list," I replied.

He scanned it and shook his head. "Nope."

I cursed Doyle inwardly, already reaching into my pocket to call Benetti.

"But maybe the little lady is on the list," he added, his eyes locked on the curve of Hope's breasts before licking his lips suggestively.

I let my hand trail down Hope's back and grabbed her hip, pulling her toward me in a possessive gesture.

"Hope Myers?" she tried, leaning into me, and despite the dangerousness of the situation, I could not help but marvel at her seeking safety with me.

"Ah, yes. Hope Myers plus one."

Doyle was a dick but a smart one. He ensured that I would take her no matter what.

"Please walk in. I'll let Ronan know you're on your way."

I kept my hand on Hope's hip as we walked into the club. We fit so well together.

We followed a man through the main part of the club down to the *Den of Forbidden Pleasures,* as it was written on top of an archway.

"Please wait here; Ronan will come for you in a minute."

As we waited, a curtain opened, revealing a blond woman being roughly fucked by a large man covered in tattoos.

The corridor started to fill with the passionate cries coming from the room, and after looking for a second, Hope snorted and rolled her eyes as if the woman's cries of pleasure left her completely unaffected.

I looked down at her as she looked away, tapping her foot impatiently as she glanced to the door of Ronan's office. It made me angry at her in a very unfair way. My body reacted to that woman's pleasure but not *for* her; I couldn't care less about her sexual prowess. No, I imagined Hope—lying on my bed, her lilac hair spread across my pillow as she made similar noises with my cock so deep inside of her, she would feel me for days.

I shook my head with a sigh, adjusting myself. It was not the time and place for these kinds of thoughts.

It's never the time and place for thinking about Hope Myers! She is off-limits.

I should have just dropped it altogether, but how could she… "It doesn't do anything to you at all?" I asked before I could think better of it.

She turned toward me, an eyebrow raised. "What?"

Sure, Jiro, tell her you're a fucking perv. "Her pleasure,"

I added, pointing at the window.

She waved her hand dismissively. "She's a good actress. I'll give you that."

My frown deepened. "Why do you say that?" I glanced at the scene again, and the woman had her head back, her eyes rolled as she orgasmed. I raised an eyebrow, a smirk playing on my lips as I glanced back at Hope. "I can assure you that woman is not faking."

She shrugged, her gaze distant. "I don't care. I'm not into sex. I've never... felt that way, not like others seem to."

"You're not into..." I shook my head; I had to have misheard.

She sighed. "Jiro, I'm not going to discuss that with you. I don't like it."

I felt like the devil possessed me, and I took one step after another toward her until she had her back pressed against the wall and I was looking down at her.

I stepped closer, my voice dropping to a whisper, the confidence in my eyes challenging her. "Trust me, with the right man, you would. I saw how you reacted with just a brush of my hand, how you responded to our kiss." I brought my hand up and trailed a finger along the column of her neck. "I can confidently say, Hope, that if you were in my bed, I would make you scream in ways you've never even dreamed of."

She met my gaze challengingly. "Prove it."

"No," I let out a little too vehemently. I took a step back in surprise just as a redhead, middle-aged man who I assumed was Ronan opened the office door.

"Ah, the sister and the yakuza." He gestured us in. "I

hope you enjoyed the show."

Hope shrugged, despite the pink hue on her skin that I knew was not due to the couple having sex but just to my proximity.

"Was it for the shock factor?" she asked, walking into the office. "I'm sorry to say it was a failure."

Ronan chuckled, rounding his desk and gesturing to the seats across from it.

"So, Doyle said you had some questions. I'm listening," he said, resting his hand on his soft belly and looking at Hope.

Hope threw me a side look, and I jerked my head toward Ronan. He wanted her to lead the conversation.

I sighed, extending her the gold coin.

"It's about my brother, Leo." She put the coin on his desk. "He's been gone for over a week, and that's the only lead I have."

Ronan nodded, pulling the coin closer to him. "It's a real one."

I inhaled deeply and rolled my eyes. "We know," I let out on a loud exhale.

"I'm not sure what I can tell you that you don't already know. We've not seen Leo Myers in a while, and he would not be welcome without this," he added, tapping his finger on the coin.

I had a lot of experience in interrogation; we could even say I was a master in the art, and I recognized political cant from a mile away. The only way to make him talk was to tap into his price.

"You know, I have to say, I'm quite impressed with the

way you're running this club. It's far more inclusive than Boston is. Good on you for being more open," I offered with a smile.

He frowned, turning slightly on his seat to face me, taking the bait I threw his way. "What do you mean?" he snorted. "Don't you know how expensive the joining fees are?"

I leaned back in my chair, extending my legs and crossing them at the ankles. " I know that, but for Boston, money is not enough; you need a name and connection, and, no offense to Hope here, Leo Myers is a nobody."

Hope was far from being a nobody, at least not to me. Fuck, it was the opposite! The woman had the potential to become my everything.

"But it's all good though. I think it makes sense for smaller clubs to be less exclusive."

Ronan's mouth ticked up with annoyance. "Is that what you think? Well, I'll ask you to rethink that. By accepting Leo Myers's money, we've got a direct line to Manuel Valdez."

Gotcha!

His eyes widened a little at his slipup, and his previous placid, almost amused expression turned into a scowl. "I think we're done here."

"No, I don't think we are. Doyle said we could ask what we want about Leo Myers."

"He did, but he also said as long as it doesn't impact other clients' privacy."

"Is Valdez a client?"

Ronan stood up. "You can go now."

I mirrored his movement, but Hope remained on her chair. "No, please. I—You're the only lead we have. Mr. Ronan, please."

He looked at her, and his face softened. Yes, it was impossible not to melt when looking at Hope's deep-blue eyes and angelic face. "I don't know anything more, little one, but I can make a promise to you. If your brother shows up, I'll call you day or night, okay?"

"But…" She turned toward me, her eyes helpless.

I smiled down at her and extended my hand. "We have what we need, Hope, I promise."

She threw me a hesitant look before staring at my hand. *Trust me.*

My heart filled with joy when she slipped her hand in mine, albeit a little hesitantly, and I pulled her up.

"Thank you for your time, and thank Doyle for me," I added, automatically pulling Hope against me. It was not necessary, but as with everything with Hope Myers, once I tried, I was addicted, and I loved having her body molded against mine.

Ronan nodded before letting his eyes trail up Hope's body before going back down, resting on her bare thighs.

"If you're ever looking for a job…" He trailed off, and Hope's mouth tipped down with disgust.

I pursed my lips, trying to ignore how his look and comment made me feel, and opened the door, but once she was out, I thought better of it and closed it, leaving her in the corridor.

I turned around, resting my back on the door, and channeled all the darkness I had inside me.

"Tell you what, *Ronan*. You look at her that way again or make those allusions one more time, and I can tell you that Doyle or no Doyle, I will cut out your tongue and make you swallow it before gouging your eyes out and leaving you to rot on the floor. I've done it before, and I don't mind doing it again."

He paled and took a step back, his previous bravado gone.

"Jiro!" Hope called, knocking on the door.

"I am and *always* will be an executioner. Remember that, Ronan," I added quickly before opening the door. "Ready?"

She looked flustered and overly annoyed as she scowled at me.

I grabbed her hand and started down the corridor toward the exit.

"What was that about?" she hissed as we took the metal stairs back up to the main part of the club.

"I needed to remind him who he was dealing with."

"And who's that?" she asked, stopping on the last step, refusing to move.

"Death," I replied, opening the door and pulling her forward.

I know my words probably scared her, but I had no time to look at her face. We needed to get out of this place, and even if I hated scaring her, at least it made her move again.

As soon as we hit the busy street, she pulled her hand out of mine and crossed her arms on her chest.

"What was that all about?" She glowered; fuck, she was beautiful. "We came here and left with nothing."

I looked around the street for a second, looking for both a taxi and some ears that may be lurking around.

"We do have something," I replied quite evasively, but as I glanced at what I suspected was supposed to be her best death glare, I sighed. "We know that your brother is obviously pretty much alive and is much higher in the Valdez organization than I could have expected." Or from what I was able to find online.

"Is that a good thing?"

I looked at her and grimaced. "For him? Probably. For us?" I shrugged. "I'm not certain yet."

"What are we doing now?"

"Now? I'm waiting for Oda to get here, and I am getting a meeting with Valdez."

"*We* are. You said you'll do it with me."

"No, *I* am. And I said that as long as it was safe. Valdez *is not* safe."

"I want to come."

"You won't. End of discussion." I shook my head as irritation grew at the stubborn woman by my side. I needed to get her home now. I looked at the taxi station. "Come on, let me take you home."

She looked down at her dress and shook her head. "No, I'll take a taxi. I'm not dressed for getting on your bike."

I would have loved to disagree, and I probably would have if there were less baggage between us. I definitely would have liked her spread on my bike. I would have loved to get a peek at the type of underwear she'd worn under this sexy outfit.

"We're not taking my bike. We'll grab a taxi," I said,

raising my arm to call one.

"What about your bike?"

"I'll come pick it up later."

The taxi stopped in front of us, and I opened the door before extending my hand to help her in.

She ignored my hand and climbed in, flashing me with the red lace of her underwear, temporarily freezing my brain.

She grabbed the handle once she sat. "I'll go home by myself. I don't need a keeper, Jiro Saito. I needed an ally, and it's clearly not what you are." She pulled the door closed, and I watched it drive off, my cock in a semi with only the piece of red lace in my mind.

Fuck my life.

NINE

Hope

I couldn't even say I was angry at Jiro, not really. No, I was disappointed and hurt at his rejection.

He had no idea how difficult it had been for me at the club to be up front the way I'd been. Sex was… a sensitive subject for me, to say the least, and the way I offered myself to him and how he almost recoiled.

You're nothing more than a cold, frigid bitch. Jared's voice rang in my ear, and I twisted uncomfortably in my seat, feeling the pain and discomfort that all physical intimacy with him had caused.

"More coffee?"

"What?" I blinked, turning toward the tired-looking waitress holding a glass coffeepot in her hand.

"Your cup has been empty for a while." She nodded toward the white cup in front of me. "Do you want more coffee?"

"Yes, thank you." I honestly didn't know why I said that—I didn't even like black coffee, but it was the cheapest thing on the menu, and after my night shift at the emporium, I needed caffeine while I waited, staring at the seedy bar across the street until Pedro appeared.

Jiro cut me out of the investigation without consideration, and I decided to ignore him, too. Would he approve of what I was doing? Probably not. Did I care? Infuriatingly so. But would I do it anyway? You bet I would!

I was going to see Pedro and ask him to take me to Valdez. Let's see how Jiro would like it if I bested him.

It was stupid to think that he would see me as his equal or that he would even get past who I was or what I represented, and this was why I could not really be mad at him. I was the reminder of what he considered his biggest sin. How could he ever see past that?

Pedro finally arrived at the bar. I grabbed my bag, put ten dollars on the table, and began to slide out of the booth.

The last thing I expected was a young Asian man

approaching and suddenly sliding into the seat across from me. Startled, I looked up, my eyes narrowing at his audacity.

"Um, excuse me?" I stammered, my irritation palpable.

The man gave me a grin that was almost too wide. As if he had a secret. "Chill out, Hope. We're all friends here."

I narrowed my eyes at him, detailing his appearance. He was much younger than Jiro, probably closer to my age, and was wearing his hair up in a bun and shaved to the sides, a little like Jiro; however, the similarities stopped there. He was dressed like a grunge nineties kid reliving his past glory. He wore a pair of ripped jeans, Reebok hi-tops, a faded band T-shirt, and an oversized plaid shirt.

"And you are?"

He leaned back, acting all mysterious with a taunting smile. "Oda. Just call me Oda."

My eyebrows shot up. "Oda? Like, the random dude who just plopped into my coffee time?"

He chuckled, a low rumble that grated on my nerves. "Coffee time… Right. Whatever you were about to do, sweet cheeks, I'll ask you to reconsider."

I crossed my arms, my patience wearing thin. "And what do you want, Oda?"

He leaned forward, his voice dropping to a near whisper. "I'm here to keep an eye on you."

Jiro! I cursed internally. I stared at him, not sure if I should be amused or annoyed. "Keep an eye on me? Seriously? Am I, like, a criminal or something?"

He shook his head, that annoying grin still plastered on his face. "Not a criminal. Just someone who obviously needs a bit of looking after."

My irritation bubbled up, and I couldn't help the sarcasm that dripped from my words. "Oh, how nice of you! But let me guess, I'm not allowed to cross the street by myself either, right?"

Oda's grin widened as he pointed to the bar across the street. "Listen, when I see where you were planning to go? Abso-*fucking*-lutely."

I let out a huff of exasperation. "Right. So he's sent you here to babysit me now. It's getting too boring for him?" I had to admit that no matter how irritated I was, this one stung quite a bit, too. Jiro was now delegating my safety.

Oda's laughter was genuine this time. "Not exactly babysit, more like… ensure you don't stumble into trouble."

"I can take care of myself. I've been doing it for years."

He leaned in again, his eyes twinkling. "I believe that. But you see, Jiro's a bit overprotective when it comes to you."

I fought back a snort. "Overprotective? And this is why he sent a Nirvana fanboy to keep me safe… No offense."

Oda chuckled with a shrug. "None taken, Nirvana's lit, and he does care about you, you know." He tapped his knuckles on the table. "Him assigning me to you is a huge statement of that."

I sighed, my annoyance softening in resignation. "And why is that?"

He shrugged again. "It just is."

I let out a growl of frustration. "See! That, right there!" I pointed an accusing finger toward him. "The half-truth, the… the…" I waved my hand dismissively. "He's not letting me be part of finding Leo, and he's just treating me like I'm a waste of space stuck to his feet… A hindrance."

Oda's grin faltered for a moment, and I relished in that small victory. "You're reading this all wrong, and you know what? I'll tell you more. You think you know the world your brother is in, but you don't. It's nothing like the films or the TV shows. They will not care if you're cute or innocent. I'll be honest. Having you around in this investigation would actually help. Using you as bait to get to Valdez or your brother would be the fastest way, but Jiro…" He shook his head. "He doesn't accept the truth yet."

"Which is?"

He smiled. "You are not just anyone for him, and by making me come here, he admitted to everyone… if not to himself. So you see, if you're so determined to walk in there…" He pointed at the window again. "I won't stop you, but I'll come with you, and then Jiro will ride my ass and not in the way I like."

I slumped back in my seat in defeat. "So what do I do now, huh? Just stay put and wait for the men to save the day?"

"Oh no." Oda's smile turned wolfish. "Now we help Jiro understand."

"Understand what?"

"What it would mean to let you slip away."

***

I stood in front of the mirror, my reflection staring back at me with a mixture of excitement and uncertainty. The dress I was wearing was far more daring than anything I had ever worn before—a black number that hugged every curve and left little to the imagination. Oda's words echoed in my mind, urging me to take a bold step, to push Jiro's buttons a little. It was crazy, reckless even, but something in me wanted to take that leap.

As I looked at myself, doubts gnawed at my confidence. Was this really the way to get Jiro's attention? Dressing provocatively, going to a club owned by the Valdez cartel? Stepping into the lion's den to both sniff my brother or Valdez out and drive Jiro to act on whatever was stopping him? It did sound a little simplistic, but then again, if Jiro's protectiveness was anything to go by, maybe a little jealousy was exactly what he needed.

Taking a deep breath, I pushed those doubts aside and walked out of my apartment. My mother was spending the night at the center, and I had the whole night to myself— something that had not happened in a very long time.

The night air was cool against my skin, sending a shiver down my spine. I hailed a cab and gave the name of the club Oda had given me. As we drove, I couldn't help but second-guess myself. What was I doing? Was this really going to work? Was I just making a fool out of myself? Was it dangerous for me to go there and ask the questions Oda suggested?

He assured me it was safe, that even if the club belonged to the cartel, it was not HQ for any of his operations. But I couldn't help but worry I was potentially creating more trouble for Jiro, and a hint of guilt appeared, tainting my determination a little.

The thumping music greeted me as I stepped out of the cab. The club was alive with colorful lights and pulsating energy. Taking another deep breath, I walked in. The bass of the music vibrated through me as I slowly looked around, not really sure what I was looking for.

I found a spot at the dimly lit bar, the soft hum of conversations and the clinking of glasses creating a soothing background noise. The sensation of eyes on me was undeniable, and I knew it wasn't just my imagination. Men and women alike were stealing glances, their gazes lingering on the daring dress that I had chosen. It was both empowering and unnerving, and for a moment, I felt a surge of self-consciousness. I leaned against the bar, casting a careful eye over the array of colorful cocktails on the menu. My mind raced as I considered the best way to approach the situation, the words I needed to say hovering on the tip of my tongue.

A young-looking bartender sidled up to me with a charming smile. His sandy-blond hair fell just above his bright-blue eyes, and he had that mischievous twinkle that usually accompanied flirtatious interactions. My heart fluttered—I hadn't flirted much before, and I hoped it looked far smoother than it would feel.

"Hey there, gorgeous," he purred, leaning in slightly. "What can I get you tonight?"

I matched his flirtatious tone, giving him a coy smile. "Surprise me. Something sweet and dangerous."

He chuckled, his fingers deftly working as he mixed the ingredients. I couldn't help but notice the way his gaze lingered on me, his attention clearly focused. I watched, feigning interest, as he poured the vibrant concoction into a glass, his fingers brushing against mine as he handed it over.

"Here you go, lovely," he said with a wink, and I couldn't

deny the flutter in my chest at his attention. Flirting might not have been my forte, but it seemed to be working—or maybe he was just good at his job.

I took a sip of the cocktail, the sweetness dancing on my taste buds. Gathering my courage, I leaned a bit closer, making sure to maintain eye contact. "I'm Hope, by the way. Do you happen to know my brother? His name's Leo, Leo Myers."

His confident demeanor wavered slightly, his eyes flickering with a hint of discomfort. "I'm afraid I don't."

I decided to push a little harder. "He works with Valdez, you know, your boss."

The flirty look in his eyes turned serious, his smile fading. "I really don't know what you're talking about."

And with that, he walked away, leaving me alone at the bar. I let out a slow breath, both relieved and pleased with the outcome. It seemed that the connection between Valdez and my brother was known, at least on some level. My heart raced with anticipation and nervousness—I was one step closer to unraveling the mystery of my brother's disappearance.

Now, I just needed to tackle the more challenging part of my plan—making Jiro jealous enough to reveal his true feelings. As I sipped my cocktail, I couldn't help but feel a rush of determination. If I could bait a cartel boss, I could surely make a complicated man like Jiro Saito take notice. It was a challenge I was more than willing to accept.

The thumping music continued to fill the air around me as I sipped my drink, lost in my own thoughts. Suddenly, a familiar figure appeared by my side, swaying his hips in a way that was both hilarious and strangely enticing. Oda, with that mischievous grin on his face. His energy was infectious, and I couldn't help but smile more genuinely now.

"Play along," he whispered, his warm breath brushing against my neck. His proximity sent a shiver down my spine, but I nodded, ready to see where this was going. He trailed his nose along the length of my neck. "Our man is seething," he whispered just as he reached my earlobe.

He grabbed my hand to help me off my seat and led me onto the dance floor. With his hands confidently finding their place on my hips, I couldn't help but steal a glance toward the bar. Jiro was there, his gaze locked onto us with irritation and something else—something I couldn't quite decipher. His drink remained untouched, his jaw clenched.

Oda's touch was light but sure, guiding me in a playful and alluring dance. I let myself get lost in the music, in the moment, all the while aware of Jiro's eyes on us. Oda's hands slid lower, his touch growing more intimate as the song's tempo increased.

Just as I was starting to wonder how much longer we could keep up this act, I felt a presence behind me. Oda's hands disappeared as quickly as they had come, and I turned to find Jiro standing there, his gaze locked onto me with an intensity that took my breath away.

Without a word, Jiro's hand found its place on my waist, his touch possessive and firm. He pulled me against him, his body moving in sync with mine as if he had been dancing beside me all along. The contrast between Oda's playful approach and Jiro's commanding hold was electrifying.

His touch was unlike anything I had ever experienced. It sent waves of heat through me, igniting a fire that had been smoldering beneath the surface and causing my panties to dampen in a way that only he could.

His fingers traced the curves of my body, leaving a trail of sensation in their wake. Every move. Every touch. Felt intentional, like he was trying to convey something that words couldn't express.

As the music pulsed around us, our bodies moved in a primal and intimate rhythm. My heart raced, my breath hitched, and all I could focus on was Jiro—his spicy scent, his touch, the way his eyes bore into mine with a hunger that mirrored my own.

"Do you think it's smart to tease a man like me?" he growled, his words laced with a restrained fury that sent shivers down my spine. I held his gaze, refusing to let my bravado waver despite the torrent of lust that his intense eyes ignited within me.

I met his challenge head-on. "It seemed that you didn't care," I retorted boldly, my heart pounding loudly in my chest. "You don't want me. I found a man who does."

His grip on my arm tightened, and suddenly, I was flush against his chest, his proximity sending my senses into overdrive. Heat pooled in my stomach and between my legs as my body betrayed my bravado. His nearness lit a fiery ache that I struggled to suppress.

He leaned in, his voice low and dangerous. "Do not play this game, Hope," he growled, his words a warning of the storm that raged beneath his composed surface. "You think you can handle me? You think you can deal with the consequences of having me?"

I took a deep breath, determined to stand my ground despite the trembling that had taken over my limbs. "Yes," I replied, my voice unwavering, my eyes locked onto his in a challenge. "But I think you're just too scared to let me prove it to you."

And then, just as the tension reached its peak, Jiro's hand slipped to the back of my neck, his fingers tangling in my hair. He pulled me closer, his lips hovering dangerously close to mine. My heart pounded in my chest, my senses overwhelmed by the sheer intensity of the moment.

"You want a yakuza?" he growled, his voice low and husky. "I'm the only one you'll ever have."

Before I could respond, his lips crashed against mine in a kiss that was fierce, passionate, and completely consuming. The world around us faded away, leaving only the two of us in this heated embrace. It was a kiss that spoke of longing, of pent-up desire, and of a connection that went far deeper than words.

As his lips left mine, he looked at me with a fire in his eyes that matched my own. "Be careful what you wish for, Hope," he murmured, his words a warning and a promise.

His hand slipped around mine, his grip firm as he pulled me through the pulsating crowd of the club.

My heart raced, my breath coming in short gasps as I struggled to keep up with his determined stride. "Where are we going?" I managed to ask, my voice breathless with exertion.

He glanced at me, his gaze intense as he continued leading me through the maze-like pathways of the club. "My hotel," he replied, his voice low and rough, sending shivers down my spine. Each word was laced with a promise that left me both exhilarated and unnerved.

He didn't say anything more as we stepped out into the cool night air as he hailed a cab, and I didn't need words to know that something had shifted between us—something irrevocable and electrifying.

With his hand still wrapped around mine, he pulled me into the waiting taxi, the promise of a night that would change everything hanging heavily in the air.

As the taxi sped through the city, I stole glances at Jiro, his profile illuminated by the passing streetlights.

"Why now?" I asked to break the silence.

"If you're that determined to go to hell with me, no matter the warning," he began, his voice a low murmur that held a dangerous edge, "then I'll show you. I'll show you all the pleasure you can give and take."

His words hung in the air, charged with an intensity that left me breathless. I could feel the weight of his desire, his raw need, and it both terrified and enticed me. I was on the edge of a precipice, about to plunge into the unknown with a man whose darkness matched my own.

"You're a trial for my sanity, Hope Myers," he continued, his tone unwavering. "If I need to add more black marks to my soul for having you, then so be it." His gaze locked onto mine, his eyes burning with a fierce determination that sent my heart into overdrive. "I'm done fighting it, Hope."

His words echoed in the night, a declaration of surrender to the magnetic pull between us.

He leaned toward me. "It's you and me right now," he

whispered, his voice a seductive murmur against my ear, "and tomorrow? Well, come what may."

TEN

Jiro

Stepping into the dimly lit hotel room, my heart pounded in my chest as I looked at Hope, my eyes trailing down her back to her perfectly shaped bottom molded like a second skin by her dress.

She was standing there, a vision of temptation

personified, her eyes locked onto mine with a mix of apprehension and desire. Every fiber of my being was on fire, a battle raging within me that I wasn't sure I could win.

A part of my conscience was still screaming at me to do the right thing, to walk away from the edge of this precipice before I fell into a darkness from which there was no return. I knew, deep down, that nothing good could come of this. That my past, *our* past, was a minefield of pain and destruction and that involving her would only lead to more heartache.

But then I remembered when Oda had called me to tell me that he had followed her to a club owned by Valdez himself. The fear that had clenched my gut at that moment was a stark reminder that danger lurked around every corner, and I would do anything, even bleed, to protect her from it. I also remembered the burning jealousy that had surged through me as I watched her flirt with the barman and as I saw her dance with Oda. At that moment, I realized how potent my feelings for her were.

What had the years of sacrifice, of doing what was considered the right thing, what society and my own sense of duty demanded, ever brought me? What had I gained from it? A life of isolation, of darkness, of pain. And now, here was the one thing that could bring light into that darkness, the one person who could be my salvation.

I looked at Hope, my gaze unwavering, and made a decision. For once, I would take what I truly wanted. I would let go of the reins that held me back, the chains of morality and responsibility that bound me. She was my *ikigai*, my reason for being, and no matter how much I fought it, the truth was undeniable.

I wanted her. *Needed* her. And if I had only this one night, I would take it. I would take her. I remembered the burning jealousy, the fear of losing her to someone else, and the realization that life was short and uncertain.

I wanted to lay down the weapons I'd carried for so long, to shed the armor that had become a part of me. For once, I wanted to be just Jiro, a man who could find solace, happiness, and love in the arms of the woman who had become my everything.

My heart raced as I stepped closer to her, the desire burning within me almost unbearable. I couldn't help but let my fingers trace the delicate curve of her collarbone before hooking onto the strap of her dress. In her eyes, I saw the apprehension again and even a hint of fear, and for a moment, I hesitated.

As I began to pull away, seeing the uncertainty etched across her features, her hand caught mine, stopping me. She pressed a soft kiss to my palm, sending a jolt of warmth through me.

"Are you sure you want this?" I asked softly, my voice laden with concern. "Nobody is forcing you. If you are having second thoughts, I…" My fingers started to slip away, but she held on, her touch grounding me in this fragile moment.

Her lips pressed against my palm again, and my heart swelled at her conviction. "No, I want this," she replied, her voice steady but her eyes betraying a mixture of emotions. "I have no doubt about that, but I'm afraid."

I was taken aback. Afraid? My mind raced, thinking of

all the possibilities that could be causing her fear. But her next words cut through my thoughts, raw and honest, and a pang of sympathy tugged at my chest.

"I'm afraid of not liking it," she continued, her gaze dropping to the floor. "I've only had one lover before, and it was a chore. I hated it."

Her words struck me deeply. The vulnerability in her confession was a sharp contrast to the brave exterior she often showed. I reached out, my fingers slipping under her chin to gently lift her head, forcing her to meet my gaze. Her blue eyes, glistening with unshed tears, held a truth that shook me to my core.

"Hope." I brushed my thumb against her cheek. "I would never hurt you. I want you to know that."

She swallowed, her gaze flickering away for a moment before returning to mine. The emotions in her eyes were a tempest I understood all too well.

"I never felt for Jared what I feel for you," she confessed, her voice barely above a whisper. "He never affected me the way you affect me. And I need to enjoy this, Jiro. It's you. If I don't, my heart would break for all that you and I could have been."

Her words hung in the air, heavy with unspoken desires and regrets. I felt a surge of tenderness for her, a fierce protectiveness I hadn't known was possible. Without another word, I closed the distance between us, my arms wrapping around her, holding her as if I could shield her from all the pain and uncertainty that life had thrown her way.

"Hope," I murmured against her hair, my lips brushing

softly against her ear. "You deserve to be loved in every way that brings you joy, not pain. And I swear to you, I will make sure that you experience nothing but pleasure, nothing but the depth of what you deserve."

She leaned into my embrace, her fingers curling into the fabric of my shirt as if holding on to me like an anchor in a storm. And in that moment, as our heartbeats seemed to synchronize, I knew that despite the darkness that had haunted me, despite the battles I had fought and the demons I had faced, there was a chance for something beautiful, something real.

As my lips met hers, a surge of emotions rushed through me like a tidal wave. It was a kiss fueled by my longing, regrets, and desires, finally breaking free. Her soft lips pressed against mine, igniting a fire that had been smoldering beneath the surface for far too long.

Her fingers tangled in my hair, pulling me closer, and I responded eagerly, deepening the kiss. Our breaths mingled, and the world around us faded into insignificance. At that moment, it was just her and me, lost in the intensity of our connection. As I let my hands trail down her body, I grabbed the hem of her short dress, pulling it up, only breaking the kiss to toss it on the floor.

I took a step back, my breathing ragged, and studied her in her black lacy underwear and strapless bra.

She was stunning, the kind of goddess that made you fall on your knees and weep just for a chance to get a taste of heaven, and right now, she was all mine.

I stared at the swell of her breasts that moved fast with her rapid breathing and removed my shirt, revealing, this time fully, my tattooed chest to her. I wanted to feel her skin against mine, her milky softness against my rendered flesh.

I walked back to her silently, far too aroused and nervous to actually talk. I had never felt nervous before sex, not even my first time. But as apprehensive as she was with her desire to enjoy it, I was just as apprehensive to make sure I made it pleasurable for her.

I reached behind her, undoing her bra, and pulled her against me. I closed my eyes with a sigh. Her skin against mine didn't just feel nice; it was like a balm soothing all my scars, both physical and emotional.

I remembered Hoka's demented explanation about Violet and the way it felt when he touched her. I thought I understood, but I didn't—not when I was now experiencing it firsthand.

I trailed my hand the length of her spine as she shivered in my arms.

"It will be good, I promise," I whispered. "It's you and me."

She didn't reply but turned her face to kiss my chest, resting her lips on the scar just above my pectoral. The scar that was caused by the gunshot I'd taken trying to protect Anna that fateful day. But before I could get lost in the painful memories, she licked the metal of my nipple barbell, making me hiss.

My cock, which was already in a semi, hardened fully as her hot tongue licked again.

I let out a groan and took a step back, already feeling the control slipping through my fingers. I needed to take back control. I needed to make tonight about her, her pleasure; she was the priority because I didn't want any apprehension, any fear in her eyes the next time I touched her, only anticipation for the pleasure I was about to give her.

Next time... There might not be a next time. My brain chimed, but I smothered it, kissing Hope deeply as I kneaded her perfect right breast with my hand.

"God, woman," I growled.

"Jiro!" she squealed as I reached down, swept her off her feet and laid her down on the bed.

I stayed on the side of the bed but leaned down to suck one of her pink nipples into my mouth.

She gasped, burying her hand in my hair. "Jiro…" she breathed.

I let it out with a loud pop and walked to the foot of the bed, reaching for her underwear. "Raise your hips for me, sweetheart."

She looked at me with more apprehension despite the desire as she raised her hips. A sign of trust I was not taking lightly.

I spread her quivering legs and looked at her glistening flesh, swollen with desire, and licked my lips in anticipation.

I kneeled at the foot of the bed and pulled her toward me.

She gasped as she raised up on her forearms. "What are you doing?" she breathed, her face crimson.

"Feasting," I replied and cocked my head to the side. "You've done that before, haven't you?"

She turned even redder as she shook her head, and I wanted to kill the piece of shit she called her ex.

I wanted to know what made her think sex was painful and not enjoyable. I wanted to know why her piece-of-shit ex made her believe she was not cut out for pleasure, that she was broken, and I started to piece it together. That man had been nothing more than a selfish taker, but I was going to prove to her now that there had never been anything wrong with her.

I reached into my pocket for a small white box and was surprised to find a box of condoms too. I had not planned for sex, but that was so perfect I didn't question it further. I got the white box out and she narrowed her eyes. Curiosity temporarily replaced her discomfort.

"What is that?"

I smiled. "I have to rise to the challenge, sweet girl. I made a bet with myself that I'd give you at least five orgasms before the sun was up."

"I—" She stopped, widening her eyes as I stuck my tongue out and screwed in my tongue piercing.

I smiled as I wrapped my arms around her tensed thighs, making sure to keep them open, and pulled her down just a little more.

"Jiro you—" She let out a startled cry as I swiped my tongue up her enticing flesh, ensuring that the ball of my piercing pressed against her swollen clit.

I repeated the ministration, adding more pressure this time, and she let out a broken moan as I felt her body relax and her head fall heavily against the pillow.

I kept lapping at her, alternating speed and pressure, learning her body's reactions and slowly getting lost in her moans of pleasure.

Everything about her was made to lure me. She was my own siren, and I would gladly drown just to be by her side.

As I increased my speed, her hips started to move up and down, trying to ride my face, seeking a release she'd never known in the arms of a man.

I smiled as her moaning became louder, and she chanted my name. And then, just as her hip movement became more erratic, I pressed my piercing against her clit while pushing two fingers inside her wet heat, and she came shouting my name.

I licked lazily until she came down from her orgasm, and she let her legs fall to the side, completely spreading herself and far too satiated to care… as it should be.

I stood up, licking my lips. "That's one," I said as I unbuttoned my pants.

She looked at my hands, her eyes a little hazy as she followed my gesture, and her eyes widened a little when I pushed my pants and underwear down, revealing my fully erect, pierced cock.

"It was true," she whispered, keeping her eyes on it.

"Uh-huh." I grinned as her expression was more curious than concerned now as she took in the three barbell piercings in the underside of my penis.

I stepped out of my discarded pants, grabbed one of the condoms and rolled it on my length, never breaking eye contact before walking back toward the bed, pushing her up before kissing and licking my way up her body.

"D-does it hurt?" she asked in a broken moan as I rolled my tongue in her belly button.

"No, not anymore." I kissed my way up her stomach,

then her rib cage, until I reached her delicious breasts again. "No, sweetheart. Now it's only pleasure for you and for me," I added before sucking a nipple in my mouth, biting it gently before rolling my tongue around it.

She buried her hands in my hair before scraping her short nails on my scalp. "Your tongue is delicious."

I smiled around her nipple before letting it go. "Wait until you try my cock," I replied before giving the same attention to her other nipple.

I trailed my lips up her neck before kissing her deeply, getting lost in her mouth as my cock brushed against her wetness.

I grabbed it as I kept kissing her and pushed the head in. She immediately tensed up, making me want to murder her stupid ex all over again.

I broke the kiss. "Relax, sweetheart. You'll love it, I promise."

She rested her hand on my cheek and gave me a watery smile. "It's okay if I don't like it. It's not your fault."

"Yes, it would be," I replied, pushing a little more inside of her. "A man who doesn't know how to properly use his toy is just a boy."

"Just go for it. It won't change anything."

"You're wrong, *koibito*. It changes everything." I pushed a bit more, and she let out a little gasp at the first barbell. I pulled back and pushed in again, going in and out with shallow thrusts, pushing in a little more with every forward movement. I kept my eyes on her face, making sure there was no pain there.

The rational part of me knew it was going to be fine;

she was built for me, and I was constructed for her. She was my *ikigai,* after all, even if it was not something I intended to tell her.

I kept my thrusting slow, and it took most of my willpower. It was so difficult not to simply settle in her tight heat.

At my last thrust, I was in to the hilt, and I let out a little huff of relief as all I saw was a marvel and the most terrifying love.

She smiled a little and raised her hips. "Oh! I'm so…"

"So?" I encouraged, detailing her face and the adorable little frown that appeared between her brows.

She raised her hips again. "I'm so… high," she replied as if she could not pinpoint how she felt.

Make that two of us, koibito. The intensity of the pleasure of just tasting her, being inside her, was like nothing I had ever experienced before. It felt like I'd just reached the door of heaven, and I knew I'd die a happy man.

She moved her head to kiss my shoulder, and I started to thrust a bit more forcefully, pulling my cock out completely and sinking back to the hilt. She let out a long moan, and I grinned against her neck.

Yes, that's what I wanted to hear. I picked up the pace, encouraged by her cries of pleasure, her hip movements, and the way she hooked her leg around my hip to deepen the angle of penetration, and finally let go of the little control I had left, getting lost in the heaven of her arms.

I was losing myself with her; it was more than an addiction. It was just her—she was everything.

I was getting close, too close, too fast, and the only

reassurance was that her cries were getting louder, her hip movements just as erratic as mine.

"Rub your clit for me, sweetheart," I huffed as I felt my balls tighten, knowing I was a couple of movements away from exploding in pleasure.

She shook her head with a broken moan but still reached between us, and just as her fingers brushed her swollen clit, she opened her eyes wide and arched her back, her mouth opening in a silent cry. Fuck, she was absolutely stunning as she orgasmed.

She tightened almost painfully around my length, and I had no choice but to let go and follow her into the most powerful orgasm I'd ever had. I could feel it all the way to my bones, and I knew that nothing could ever compare to sex with Hope.

But it was not just sex, was it? No, it was love—I made love to her; I got lost in her in ways I would have never allowed with anyone else.

I fell on top of her, and she wrapped herself around me as if she wanted to keep me deep inside of her. As if I ever wanted to move from the delicious bliss her body was.

She kissed the side of my head. "Thank you," she said with a voice far more emotional than I would have expected.

I was about to turn my head when she continued. "Thank you for showing me I was not broken. Thank you for showing me sex was pleasurable."

I turned my head and kissed the side of her neck.

"I'm a big fan of your *appendage*," she said with a low, self-conscious chuckle. "And those piercings…" She tightened her walls around my softening cock. "They're something else."

"Give me a few minutes, and then I'll show you how they feel on your tongue."

She chuckled again and let out a sigh. "I love you, Jiro Saito."

I tensed but kissed her neck. I could not say it back. It was just the heat of passion talking, her gratefulness at showing her she was not damaged. I could not reciprocate because I knew that if I did, I would never let her go.

ELEVEN

Hope

The morning light filtered through the curtains, painting the room in soft hues as I gradually awakened from a night of passion. My body felt pleasantly sore, a lingering reminder of the intensity of our lovemaking. I turned my head to the side, my heart skipping a beat as I looked at Jiro. His features were relaxed in sleep, his chest rising and falling rhythmically.

I smiled, looking at him for a while. He had kept his promise and gave me six orgasms before the sun started to rise.

Last night, I bared my heart to him, confessing my feelings even though I knew he couldn't reciprocate. And surprisingly, I didn't regret it. It was as if the weight of my unspoken emotions had been lifted, and now I could face the uncertain future with a newfound clarity.

I was not broken; Jiro had proven it, and I wanted him again and again. I closed my eyes and smiled, still feeling his hardness inside of me.

Just as I was lost in my thoughts, my phone vibrated on the bedside table, pulling me back to reality. I grabbed it, my heart skipping a beat again as I half expected it to be an issue with my mother.

"Hello?"

"Whatever you're doing, Hope, it stops now." His words hit me like a bucket of cold water, instantly pulling me out of whatever trance I was in. I sat up quickly, almost knocking the lamp off the nightstand. Beside me, Jiro stirred, his eyes blinking open as he was roused from his slumber.

I placed the phone on speaker mode and set it down on the bed, knowing that whatever my brother had to say, Jiro deserved to hear it too.

"Hope, are you there?" Leo asked, the coldness in his voice so unfamiliar.

I glanced at Jiro, my heart racing. This wasn't like Leo at all. Jiro's eyes locked with mine, his expression a mix of curiosity and concern.

"Leo, where are you?" I asked, turning toward the phone again.

"It's irrelevant," he started dismissively. "You're poking your nose in Valdez business and with that fucking yakuza!" he spat with barely veiled disgust in his voice. "Do I need to remind you what he cost us? I'm sure Anna is rolling in her grave seeing you together."

I turned back to Jiro, a mix of emotions swirling in his eyes. His face was a mask, his expression unreadable, but I knew those words had struck a deep chord within him, just as they had with me. It was like Leo's words were designed to target every ounce of guilt and pain that he carried from the past.

My hand instinctively reached out, my fingers brushing gently against his cheek in a feeble attempt to convey comfort, to let him know that his past sins were not the sum of who he was. His lips pressed against my palm, a soft kiss that sent a shiver down my spine. He left the bed, his naked form a powerful sight, and my eyes followed him as he headed toward the bathroom.

"Hope," Leo's voice snapped me back to the phone, his tone accusatory. "What do you think you're doing?"

I sat up straighter, determination welling up inside me. "You disappeared, Leo. For weeks, I thought you were..." My voice trailed off, the emotion of those weeks without him choking me for a moment. "You left without a word, without any sign of where you were. And now, you dare to call and give me orders?"

I could feel my frustration boiling over, the helplessness

of not knowing what had happened to my brother for so long. And yet, he called as if he had the right to dictate my actions, to criticize my choices. It wasn't fair, and I wasn't going to let him control me any longer.

"Think again, Leo," I retorted, my voice firm. "I'm not a child anymore. I can make my own decisions, and I'll do whatever it takes to find out what happened to you and to help our family. If you're not going to share the truth with me, then I'll find it on my own."

"Hope…" He sighed. "I am working, and this has nothing to do with you. Trust me, I'm just looking out for you."

My eyes flashed to Jiro, who was now wearing a pair of boxers, leaning against the bathroom door, frowning at the phone.

"Like you looked out for me when you used the money Jiro sent each month for your stupid club, forcing me to drop out of school?" I asked with anger.

"Is that what he told you?" He let out a little laugh. "He lied to you, Hope. Just go back to your life and let me live mine, okay? Just… BACK OFF!"

"You know what, Leo? You back off!" I shouted into the phone, my anger fueling my words as I ended the call abruptly.

Jiro approached me, his footsteps silent as he walked over and sat down on the bed. His fingers found my foot beneath the covers, squeezing it gently, a silent reassurance that he was there.

"He's lying," I said, my voice thick with frustration and anger.

"I know," Jiro replied, his tone calm and collected, a soothing contrast to my boiling temper.

"None of what he said makes any sense," I continued, my hands gesturing wildly in the air. "And where's his phone? He wouldn't have just disappeared like that, not without a word. I know my brother, and he's not that egotistical. He wouldn't have left me to worry like that; he would have said something. I know he would have!" I added defiantly.

Jiro nodded, his gaze fixed on his hand resting on my leg. "It doesn't add up."

I felt a surge of relief rushing through me. He believed me, believed in my brother's goodness despite the lies and the mystery surrounding his disappearance.

"Exactly," I said, my voice still tinged with frustration, but the weight on my chest was slowly lifting. With Jiro by my side, supporting me and understanding the turmoil I was going through, I felt stronger. More determined to uncover the truth about Leo's vanishing act.

I didn't think he realized it when his hand began to trace soothing circles on my leg beneath the cover. His touch was both comforting and electric, sending a thrill through my veins.

"You're not going to let it go, are you?"

I shook my head with a sigh, his caress on my leg not ceasing. "No, I won't."

"We'll figure it out together." His eyes held a certain intensity that sent a shiver down my spine. Then his tone softened. "How are you feeling, sweetheart?"

I understood that his question went beyond the phone call. It was about what we'd shared. I blushed, my heart racing as I met his gaze, which held a depth of emotion that sent my mind spiraling.

"I feel… better than I ever thought I could," I confessed with a shy smile, my cheeks growing warmer as I recalled the passion and pleasure of our shared night. It was like I could still feel him deep inside of me. My words trailed off, my thoughts too intimate to voice. But I didn't need to finish my sentence; he already knew how profoundly he had affected me.

Jiro let out a deep breath, a visible sign of his relief, and nodded. I noticed the tension in his body slowly melting away, and I realized how anxiously he must have been awaiting my response. It only endeared him to me even more.

"That's good. I feared that your reaction to… us might have been different in the light of day," he admitted, a rare vulnerability seeping into his words. It struck me that he was sharing a deeply private part of himself, something that he likely didn't do often.

I tilted my head slightly, puzzled by his words. Hadn't he heard me tell him that I loved him? I had said it, hadn't I? I remembered feeling him tense against me when those words escaped my lips.

I wanted to ask him what he meant by "us." It could mean so much and so little at the same time, but it seemed trivial right now. Also, I was just so high, so drunk on all the pleasure he had given me last night, that I feared the answer he would give me might deflate the happy bubble I was in.

My phone beeped, jarring me from my thoughts. I sighed, reluctantly accepting the intrusion of reality. "I need to go. I have work and my mom, you know."

Jiro nodded, his fingers trailing as he pulled the cover off my leg, his touch lingering and sending a shiver up my spine as he grabbed the arch of my foot and pulled it up to kiss the top of it. "Yes, go take a shower, and I'll call Hoka. We will need his help to meet with Valdez."

I could see that involving his friend in all this bothered him, and it made me feel guilty for dragging others into the mess. "Listen, you don't have to—"

"I know I don't have to, but I want to," he interrupted softly, his eyes unwavering as they locked onto mine.

I nodded and got out of the bed, retrieving my clothes along the way. I couldn't help but smile as I felt his burning gaze on my back, and I swayed my hips a little more than necessary as I disappeared into the bathroom.

Once inside, I started to lather some of the hotel shampoo into my hair when he slipped in behind me, his presence a magnetic pull that I couldn't resist. He pressed his chest against my back, his warmth seeping into my skin, and his fingers reached out to take over where I left off. His touch was gentle, almost reverent, as he massaged the shampoo into my hair, his fingers working through the strands. The intimacy of the moment was overwhelming, and I closed my eyes, savoring the sensation.

"I know how pro-environment you are, so I thought we might save water and shower together," Jiro's voice purred behind me.

I couldn't help but smile, still keeping my back turned to him. "Oh, do you now?" I teased, the corners of my lips lifting in amusement.

A gasp escaped me as his lips found my neck, his teeth grazing over the sensitive skin. Automatically, I sucked in my stomach, the sudden contact causing goose bumps. His arms wound around my waist, pulling me closer, and I felt the heat of his bare skin and his hard cock against my back. Despite the fact that he had seen, kissed, and licked my entire naked body, the intimate vulnerability of the moment made me self-conscious under the harsh, unforgiving fluorescent light of the bathroom.

His lips brushed against my earlobe, and his warm breath sent my senses into a frenzy. "It's only me, *koibito*. Your Jiro," he whispered, his words a gentle reassurance against the shell of my ear. I exhaled a shaky breath, releasing the tension I didn't even know I was holding.

As we stood there, the water cascading around us, I realized how fleeting this moment might be. The reality of the outside world could easily wash away this intimacy we were sharing. I was afraid that once we stepped out of this bathroom, the warmth and connection we had would fizzle out, leaving behind the distant and cold Jiro I had known before. I wasn't ready to say goodbye to this, to him, to the pleasure he had brought into my life. I wanted more, needed more.

"I want more of you," I found myself admitting, my hand reaching behind me to touch his wet cock. The sensation of his hard length under my fingers sent a jolt of desire through me, and I leaned into him, craving the feeling of him deep inside me. "When you're inside me…"

"You can have all of me… I'm ridged for your pleasure," he murmured, his voice filled with a playful charm. I could hear the smile in his words, and it tugged at my heart, knowing that what he was offering was a moment of rapture in this shower and not the forever I knew I would crave at the end of this journey.

He let his hands glide upward with a featherlight touch, his palms finally cupping my breasts, running his fingers on top of my hardened nipples before pinching them, sending a zing of painful pleasure along my body, causing moisture between my thighs.

He trailed his lips on the back of my neck, letting his right hand slide down to the throbbing part of me, spreading my slit and rubbing slowly. "Ummm, you're so wet for me, sweetheart. Tell me you like it when I'm inside you." He grazed his teeth from the curve of my shoulder to my neck and bit it softly.

"Yes…" I let out on a moan, pushing back against him.

He licked the spot he bit. "Ummm, I love the way you taste. You enjoy when I eat you, don't you?"

"I do." I rested my hand against the white tiles and looked at his strong fingers playing with the most sensitive part of me, keeping me on the edge of orgasm. "I love how you taste too. I love being on my knees for you." And that was true. I loved seeing how my mouth brought him to his knees.

He growled, pushing two fingers inside me, thrusting them back and forth slowly. I rested my other hand on the wet tiles.

He removed his hand abruptly, and I let out a pitiful whine.

"I got you; rest your foot on the edge of the tub and

hold tight, sweetheart. I'm taking you for a ride." His voice was commanding, and excitement bubbled inside me as I followed his order, lifting my leg, bracing for the sweet torture his cock was.

He murmured something in Japanese, and he gripped my hips, entering me from behind in a long, swift motion.

I let out a broken cry that was more pleasure than pain. I arched my back, my eyes rolling back at the intense pleasure of this new angle and how his piercings enhanced the friction of his length against my walls.

He stayed in me unmoving, letting me accommodate his size as he let his hand trail up my body to rest it on top of mine. He interlaced his fingers with mine, keeping our hands on the wall, and I looked at them. My heart tightened with love for this man; this simple, tender gesture in the midst of our passionate moment meant far more than anything he could have voiced.

I squeezed my walls and moaned at the sensations caused by his pierced length. It felt like it was waking every nerve of my body, making me far more sensitive to every touch.

I squeezed him again, eliciting a hiss from him. In response, he bit down on my neck, the sensation a mix of pleasure and pain, not breaking the skin but leaving behind a mark that would serve as a reminder of this moment.

"Mine." His voice, rough and possessive, rumbled against my skin, proclaiming his ownership.

In a breathless whisper, I replied, the heat of the moment intensifying my words, "Yours." I shifted against him, a silent encouragement for him to move.

Jiro started slow and deep but quickly moved to more forceful thrusts that would have made me topple over if it wasn't for the wall and his bruising grip on my hip.

"Faster," I whispered breathlessly, closing my eyes, submitting to the sensation of the hot water on my skin, his erotic grunts, his powerful hips, and his imposing cock hitting just the right spot from this new position.

He growled, increasing the speed, taking me over the edge faster than I thought possible. He joined me almost immediately after my orgasm.

A soft chuckle vibrated against my back as he wrapped his arms around me, holding me close against him. "Best shower ever," he murmured, his voice still carrying a post-passion raspiness.

I nodded, a contented smile tugging at my lips as I leaned into his embrace, my head finding the perfect spot against his shoulder. "I would never have thought I'd end up dirtier in the shower than I was before getting in," I quipped, a playful glint in my eyes. The absurdity of the situation brought a surge of laughter, and I couldn't help but feel an overwhelming sense of happiness, even in the midst of uncertainty.

Once we were dressed, Jiro and I hailed a taxi to take me back home. The transition from the private cocoon of the hotel room to the outside world felt like crossing a boundary I wasn't entirely prepared for.

When we stopped in front of my building, he asked the taxi to wait and followed me silently. As we reached my front door, I fidgeted with the strap of my purse, my mind racing with unspoken questions about where we stood now.

Jiro must have sensed my uncertainty, for he gave me a small, reassuring smile, his hand gently cupping my cheek. The warmth of his touch against my skin calmed my nerves. "Call me when you're free," he said softly, his words carrying a promise that sent a rush of joy through me. "I'll take you out for dinner."

His simple invitation filled me with a surge of happiness. He leaned down, his lips brushing against mine in a chaste kiss that held a world of unspoken emotions. Just as he was about to pull away, he murmured something in Japanese against my lips. I blinked, my heart skipping a beat as I tried to catch his words. "What did you say?" I asked, my voice barely above a whisper.

A tender smile played on his lips, and he met my gaze with a depth of feeling that left me breathless. "You're everything I want and everything I don't deserve," he confessed, his voice filled with awe and longing. The vulnerability in his eyes mirrored my own feelings.

I watched him walk back to the waiting taxi, my heart racing with happiness and uncertainty. As he got into the taxi, I found myself silently sending a prayer to whatever higher power might be listening, hoping that fate would allow me to keep my yakuza.

Jiro had been a fool last night, claiming that he was the only yakuza I could ever have. In truth, he was the only yakuza I had ever wanted, the only man I truly desired.

TWELVE

Jiro

Sitting at the café across from the bar where Valdez's crew frequented, I tried to enjoy my coffee in peace. However, that tranquility was shattered as Oda slid into the chair across from me with a grin that was nothing short of mischievous.

"Jiro, my friend, in dear need of coffee, huh?" He wiggled his eyebrows, jerking his head toward the cup I was holding. "I guess someone didn't get much sleep last night."

I shook my head and took a sip of the burned-out coffee that felt like heaven because I would have rather died than admit it, but I was significantly sleep-deprived, and I was not as young as the grinning idiot in front of me.

Oda leaned over the table. "So, how's life in caveman land?"

I rolled my eyes, not in the mood for his teasing. "Very funny, Oda."

He chuckled, leaning back in his chair. "Seriously, dragging Hope out of the club like that? You've got that caveman thing down to an art."

I groaned, rubbing my temples. "Can we not talk about that?"

"Ah, come on," Oda persisted, his grin widening. "It was quite the show. Had the whole place talking."

I shot him a glare. "You're impossible."

Oda laughed heartily, enjoying my discomfort a little too much. "So, how many of the pack of twelve condoms did you manage to use?"

My face heated up, and I spluttered, nearly choking on my coffee. "What? How the hell do you know about that?"

He leaned in, his voice low and conspiratorial. "Let's just say I wanted to make sure you were prepared for the night."

I stared at him in disbelief. "You're the one who put those condoms in my pocket?"

He winked. "Guilty as charged."

I shook my head, still trying to wrap my mind around it. "You planned this whole evening, didn't you? You wanted me to snap."

Oda shrugged nonchalantly. "Well, let's just say I nudged fate a bit. Had a hunch you needed a push."

I narrowed my eyes at him. "And what about you? What was your game?"

He leaned back, his expression turning more serious. "Jiro, my friend, you're a true yakuza. You're so steeped in your own code and sense of duty that you can't see happiness even when it smacks you in the face."

I frowned, his words hitting closer to home than I cared to admit. "What are you talking about?"

He leaned in, his voice low and sincere. "You care about Hope, don't you? Maybe more than you're willing to admit. But you've built this wall around yourself, thinking you're protecting her by staying away. I just thought it was time to remind you that sometimes, it's okay to let go of the warrior facade and let happiness in."

I sighed, rubbing my temples. Oda had a way of seeing through my defenses, and it was both infuriating and oddly comforting. "You meddled in my personal life, Oda. You had no right."

He chuckled, not the least bit apologetic. "Ah, but sometimes friends need to meddle, especially when they see a stubborn idiot like you getting in his own way. And with the way you're getting your panties in a bunch, I guess you used about three of those condoms."

I should have been the bigger person and just ignored his comment. After all, he was just a kid, and I had ten years on him. Yet, my male ego took over once more. "Five," I muttered.

"Five?" He slammed his hand on the table, his eyebrows raised. "Shit, man, that's impressive. Now you're putting my own record to shame."

I couldn't help but crack a smile at that. Oda was a pain in the ass, but he was also one of the few people who kept his easygoing nature despite our dark world. "Fine, you win. But next time you want to meddle, at least warn me."

He raised an eyebrow, a mischievous glint in his eyes. "What fun would that be?"

I chuckled, shaking my head. "You're unbelievable."

He grinned. "That's why you love me, Saito."

I rolled my eyes, unable to hide my smirk. "Yeah, yeah, keep dreaming. I tolerate you at best." I sighed, looking back at the bar across the street and tapping my fingers on the table.

"What's up?" he asked more seriously now.

"When do you have to get back?"

He shrugged. "You have me as long as you need me. I suspect Alessandro was quite relieved to get rid of me for a while."

I threw him a side look and snorted. "You don't say."

"What? I'm adorable!" he gasped in mock offense, resting his hand on his chest.

"And how much shit are you allowed to stir?"

Oda leaned back, his face more serious now. "I'm here to follow your lead, Jiro. Alessandro didn't forbid me anything."

I nodded, appreciating Oda's loyalty. "Good. We'll

need all the help we can get."

Oda tilted his head slightly, sensing something more. "There's something else, isn't there?"

I sighed, leaning forward. "After Hope's questioning yesterday at the club, her brother called her out of the blue. Not a caring sibling chat, but more like an order to stop poking around."

Oda raised an eyebrow. "Sounds like a charmer."

I chuckled dryly. "You have no idea."

Oda nodded in understanding, his eyes locked onto mine. "So, what's the plan now?"

I sighed, my fingers drumming on the table. "I think Valdez pushed him to call. My problem now... it's clear Hope is on their radar, and I'm concerned that she might become collateral against her brother for... whatever he's involved with."

Oda's face darkened at the mention of collateral, his jaw clenching. "That's cold."

"Valdez isn't exactly known for his warmth," I replied grimly.

Oda leaned in, his voice lowered. "So, what's your move?"

I met his gaze with determination. "I'm going to hit one of Valdez's strongholds. The bar across the street—it's practically a base for his crew. I'm going in with the yakuza clan tattoo on display. Maybe rough up a couple of his guys, just enough to get back to Valdez and make him open a direct line to me."

Oda's lips curled into a sly grin. "That's a dangerous game, Jiro. Even for you. I never knew you were a kamikaze."

I smirked back at him. "Well, I've never been one to shy away from danger." And for Hope Myers? I'll brave the fires of hell itself.

***

The air inside the bar was thick with a mixture of smoke, sweat, and an undercurrent of tension. The dim, flickering fluorescent lights did little to mask the dinginess of the place, and the sticky floor seemed to cling to my shoes with each step. It was the kind of establishment that thrived on cheap drinks, bad decisions, and the type of clientele that preferred shadows over light.

My gaze swept over the crowd, taking in the collection of shady figures huddled in the corners, nursing their drinks. Half-naked women were strategically placed around the bar, a clear sign that this place catered to the basest desires of its patrons. I knew that the decor wasn't the reason the gang frequented this joint. It was a haven for criminal activity—a place where secrets were traded, alliances formed, and basic desires were fulfilled by ten-dollar blow jobs.

I grimaced and glanced at Oda, who was wearing the same disgusted look as I was.

The room fell into an eerie silence as we both stepped into the middle of the room, and the hostile glares of the men seated around the bar bore into me. I kept my steps steady, my eyes locked forward, giving no indication that their attention bothered me. I had walked into much more dangerous situations than this.

I spotted Pedro at the bar, nursing a drink and leering at one of the women in a way that made my stomach turn.

He noticed me, his eyes narrowing for a second before his lips curled into a smug grin. I could see the arrogance in his posture. The belief that he had the upper hand on his supposed territory.

"Pendejo," I greeted him, my voice layered with a cool confidence that I hoped would rattle him. "Fancy seeing you here."

He raised an eyebrow, not expecting to find me in his so-called domain. "Yakuza," he acknowledged, his tone laced with forced nonchalance.

I turned my head slightly, my eyes locking onto Oda's for a brief moment. "Watch my back," I muttered under my breath before sauntering over to the bar and claiming the empty stool beside Pedro.

He couldn't resist taking a jab at me. "That's a bold move, showing your face and flaunting your tattoos here. This isn't yakuza territory." His words were tinged with a mocking smirk. "Asian quarter is to the east," he added, jerking his head in that direction to emphasize his point.

I couldn't help but shake my head inwardly. The guy was so convinced of his own intelligence that he didn't realize how transparent he was. He thought this was a display of power. A territorial showdown when he was at the bottom of the food chain in any Mafia.

I leaned in a bit, my expression carefully neutral. "You really think you can lay claim to any territory, Pedro? This place? This dump? I'm not here to fight over a cesspool." I motioned to the surroundings with a dismissive wave of my hand.

Pedro's grin faltered for a moment, his bravado

slipping. I had touched a nerve, and he was trying to regain his footing. "I have connections," he sneered.

I leaned back, feigning casual indifference. "Connections? Valdez?" I laughed. "I'm not even sure he knows your name."

His irritation was palpable now, the mask of arrogance slipping further. He leaned in, his voice low and dangerous. "He won't appreciate you encroaching on his turf and bothering his man."

I chuckled softly, a hint of derision in the sound. "You really believe he cares about what happens to you?" I shook my head, letting out a mock sigh. "You're delusional, Pedro."

He clenched his jaw, clearly struggling to maintain his composure. "You're just a washed-up yakuza who's lost his edge, with far too much innocent blood on his hands to play the high and mighty." His words were like barbs, meant to provoke, but I was determined not to let him see any reaction.

I met his gaze with an unflinching stare, refusing to show that his words had any impact on me. But his last sentence struck a nerve, a reminder of the pain and guilt that still haunted me. It was true; my past was stained with actions I could never undo.

"Tell me," he continued, his voice dripping with venom, "what does it feel like to fuck the sister of the girl you killed?"

His words hit me like a punch to the gut, a rush of anger and pain surging through me. But I wouldn't let him see that he had gotten to me. I maintained my composure, my expression unwavering.

"You seem to have a lot of information for someone who's just a small-time thug," I retorted, my tone dripping with icy disdain. If he wanted to play mind games, I was more than willing to engage.

I could see a flicker of irritation cross his face, a crack in his arrogant facade. Good, he was taking the bait. As he fumed, I pulled a piece of paper from my pocket, unfolded it, and placed it on the sticky bar between us. My phone number stared back at him, a tangible challenge.

"Here's my number," I stated mockingly, pushing the paper slightly closer to him. "Give it to a grown-up with actual power so I can tell them what I need to. Maybe then, someone who can actually make decisions will get in touch."

The tense silence hung in the air, his eyes locked onto the paper, a mixture of anger and uncertainty dancing in his gaze. I didn't wait for his response; instead, I stood up smoothly, leaving him with my parting shot, and turned to walk away.

Once I was back on the other side of the road, Oda's expectant gaze met mine, waiting for an explanation. "Jiro, what was that all about? Are you sure this was a wise move?"

I couldn't help but grin as I looked at the door of the bar. "Oda, sometimes a bruised ego is the best motivator. Pedro won't be able to resist. Mocking him and his gang, daring him to have Valdez 'call the actual adult,' that's the best way to goad him into action."

"What now?" Oda asked as we walked away from the bar and toward the waterfront where my bike was parked.

I took a deep breath, feeling the weight of the situation

settling on my shoulders. "Now I need to call Hoka," I replied, my jaw tensing. It was frustrating. Pedro's taunts had struck a nerve. He was right in one sense; I wasn't the yakuza I once was, the untouchable figure I used to be. I had lost the legitimacy my position had given me.

I could feel the simmering frustration within me, filled with anger and regret. I hated how much I needed Hoka's protection now, how circumstances had changed my role from the fierce protector to the one needing protection. It was a bitter pill to swallow.

Oda appeared uneasy, his discomfort palpable. "We may need to wait a few days. Hoka is currently traveling to Japan with Sandro."

My steps faltered, and I halted in the middle of the sidewalk. "Why would Alessandro be going to Japan?" I inquired, my voice sounding confused and suspicious.

Oda shrugged nonchalantly, but his eyes betrayed a flicker of unease. Hoka hadn't mentioned anything about this when we spoke less than three days ago. This lack of trust nestled within me grew stronger, more insistent.

You're no longer part of the clan, Jiro. Yakuza business is none of your concern, the insidious voice whispered in my mind, urging me to let it go.

I shook my head—it didn't matter what Hoka and Alessandro were doing in Japan—all that mattered was that I ensured Hope's safety even once I was gone.

THIRTEEN

Hope

I stood in front of my closet, my heart pounding with excitement and nerves. My hands fumbled through the hangers, pulling out one dress after another and holding them up to the mirror. Each time, I studied my reflection, assessing how each dress made me look. How it made me feel.

"Hope dear, you look stunning in everything," my elderly neighbor, Mrs. Jenkins, gushed from the chair near my bed. She had insisted on joining me for my pre-date dress decision, her eyes lighting up with delight each time I twirled in front of her.

I smiled at her, grateful for her presence and her unwavering support. "Thank you, Mrs. Jenkins. I just want to make sure I look nice tonight."

She chuckled, her gray hair bouncing slightly as she nodded. "Oh, my dear, you'll look more than nice. You'll look radiant."

After trying on what felt like half my wardrobe, I finally settled on a beautiful white-and-lavender dress that clung to my curves in all the right places. It made me feel confident and feminine. I also knew how Jiro's eyes darkened when he could see my form, and I wanted more of that.

As I admired myself in the mirror, Mrs. Jenkins got up from her chair and approached me with a small smile. "It's good to see you so excited, sweet girl. You deserve to be happy after all..." Her voice trailed off, her face taking the faint hint of pity most people had when they knew my history of the past few years.

I fought back the sting of tears, giving her a grateful smile and a small nod. This wasn't the moment to let memories of pain cloud the excitement of what might be my first genuine adult date.

Mrs. Jenkins sighed softly, her hand finding its way to my shoulder in a reassuring squeeze. "You go have fun, dear! I'll be here with your mama, and if you don't come home… Well, that's okay, too." Her wink held a touch of conspiratorial humor.

I couldn't help but chuckle, though my cheeks flushed at the idea of spending another night with Jiro. That man had awakened desires in me that I hadn't known existed, igniting passion and a hunger that I had never imagined.

I cleared my throat, quickly shaking my head to dispel the lingering sensual thoughts that had no place in my mind right now. "Thank you, Mrs. Jenkins. Your support means the world to me."

Mrs. Jenkins patted my cheek with a grandmotherly tenderness. "Now, you go out there and knock him off his feet, dear. You deserve all the happiness in the world."

Just as her words settled into my heart, the buzzer signaling Jiro's arrival rang through the apartment. My excitement surged, and I hurried out of the room, passing through the living area. I cast a quick glance at my mother, seated in her usual chair with a knitted blanket on her lap. Her vacant gaze was fixed on the TV, her world confined to her own realm of thoughts.

I hesitated for a moment, my heart aching to have a real conversation with her, but Mrs. Jenkins's comforting words echoed in my mind. *You go, sweetheart. Go and be the young woman you deserve to be.*

With a soft sigh, I made my way to the buzzer panel and pressed the button, connecting with Jiro's waiting form downstairs. "I'll be right down," I informed him, then swiftly slipped into my comfortable Converse sneakers before rushing out of the apartment.

As I descended the steps, each heartbeat seemed to

increase my excitement. I swung open the door, and there he was, my dark hero.

The sight of him dressed all in black, looking dangerously handsome, made my heart skip a beat. His presence exuded a sense of power and confidence that was both intimidating and incredibly attractive.

"Lord, have mercy on my soul," I whispered under my breath. There was an undeniable sense of rightness. Like the missing piece of my life's puzzle was standing right in front of me.

A wide smile spread across my face as I approached him. The way his eyes roamed over my chosen outfit, his gaze lingering on my chest, hips, and legs, created a warm sensation in my chest.

"Hey," I greeted him, unable to hide the giddiness I felt as I bounced a little on my feet.

"Hey, yourself," he replied, a hint of a smirk playing on his lips.

I couldn't help but give him a playful once-over, appreciating the way his attire showcased his strong physique. "You clean up nicely," I teased, stepping closer, resting my hand on the lapel of his jacket.

He chuckled, his eyes never leaving mine. "And you look absolutely breathtaking," he replied, resting his hand on top of mine. The warmth of his callous fingers was a sweet reminder of his fingers between my legs.

My cheeks flushed at his compliment and my lurid thoughts. I bit my lip to suppress the grin threatening to take over my face. It felt so good to be desired, especially by a man who held such an aura of allure and danger.

I glanced around, half expecting to see his iconic black motorcycle parked nearby. "Where's the bike?" I asked, my tone playfully disappointed.

Jiro's grin widened, and he leaned casually against the car beside him. "I thought I'd be a gentleman for the evening."

I raised an eyebrow, unable to hide my surprise. "A gentleman, huh? Who are you, and what have you done with Jiro?"

He chuckled, his eyes twinkling with amusement. "Just thought I'd switch things up a bit."

As much as I appreciated the gesture, there was a part of me that was disappointed not to feel the rumble of his motorcycle beneath me, pressing my body against his. But then again, the idea of spending the evening with him in a more conventional manner was also appealing.

He pushed away from the black Porsche and opened the passenger door for me. As I slid into the car, his hand brushed mine, sending a jolt of electricity up my arm. I met his gaze, and there was an intensity in his eyes that made my heart race.

As he closed the car door and walked around to the driver's side, I couldn't help but think, *He's lethal, and he's mine...* at least for now.

"You know, as much as I appreciate the gentlemanly act, I don't want a gentleman. I want Jiro... My Jiro," I said, my voice carrying a note of playfulness and desire.

I hoped he remembered the raw intimacy we had shared in the shower, the way he had branded himself as mine. It was a possessive claim that had lit fire to something deep within me, and I wanted to remind him of that connection.

As he slid into the driver's seat and our gazes locked, his eyes darkened, a spark of intensity setting off between us. Without a word, he reached out, and his hand found the back of my head, his fingers tangling gently in my hair. His touch sent shivers down my spine, and I could feel the air crackling with tension.

"Be careful what you wish for," he murmured, his voice a low, husky whisper.

Before I could respond, his lips crashed onto mine with a fierce hunger that left me breathless. The kiss was passionate, fiery, and filled with all the alpha dominance that made my heart race and my knees weak. It was as if he was claiming me all over again, reminding me of his possession, his desire, and his unspoken promise.

I melted into the kiss, my fingers instinctively gripping his shirt as I pulled him closer. Time seemed to stand still as we lost ourselves in the moment, our lips and bodies pressed together, further stoking the fire that had been smoldering beneath the surface.

When he finally pulled away, our breaths mingling, I looked into his eyes, my own filled with desire, adoration, and a touch of playful challenge.

"Maybe I should be careful what *I* wish for," I teased, a mischievous smile playing on my lips.

He chuckled, his fingers gently tracing my jawline. "You have no idea."

I knew that this evening with Jiro was going to be an unforgettable ride, filled with both passion and the unpredictable allure of my yakuza.

As the car came to a halt in front of Chez Jean, one of the most upscale restaurants in town with a notorious six-month waiting list, I was left in awe. How on earth did Jiro manage to secure a reservation here? The place was practically a legend in culinary circles.

"How did you do that?" I couldn't help but ask, the surprise evident in my voice as he opened his door.

He winked at me, a mischievous glint in his eyes. "I'm a man of many secrets."

He rounded the car and engaged with the doorman, smoothly asking him to step aside. Then he was at my door, opening it with a flourish and extending his hand.

"May I?" he asked, his voice carrying a hint of playfulness as I accepted his hand. "You deserve the best, Hope Myers," he remarked, his fingers intertwining with mine, his touch both comforting and electrifying. Bringing my hand to his lips, he pressed a gentle kiss onto my knuckles, sending a shiver down my spine.

As soon as we walked in, the opulence of the restaurant took me by surprise, from the sparkling chandeliers to the plush furnishings that seemed to whisper luxury. The soft murmur of hushed conversations created an intimate ambience, and all the patrons dressed in designer clothing made me feel self-conscious. I looked down at my lilac Converses and winced.

Jiro squeezed my hand, and I looked up to see his bright smile. "You're perfect just as you are, *koibito*. You are perfect to me."

My heart squeezed in my chest, and I wanted to throw myself into his arms and kiss him senseless, but I was lucky to be stopped by the approaching hostess.

"Good evening, Monsieur Saito," she greeted Jiro, her eyes glancing briefly at me before returning to him.

How did she know his name?

"Good evening," Jiro responded with a nod, his voice carrying an air of quiet confidence.

The hostess turned her attention to me. "Mademoiselle, welcome. We have your table ready." Her French accent added to the sophisticated atmosphere of the restaurant. With a slight gesture, she led us deeper into the room, our steps guided by the soft glow of candles that adorned each table.

I caught Jiro's gaze as we walked, his eyes warm with affection. The anticipation of the night ahead mingled with the allure he exuded, creating a heady combination that left me breathless.

As we reached our table, I couldn't help but admire the elegant setting—the fine linen, the gleaming silverware, and the delicate flowers that graced the center. The hostess handed us the menus, and Jiro's ease with the French language was both impressive and a bit intimidating. He scanned the menu confidently while I struggled to decipher the elaborate descriptions of the dishes. I felt a flush of embarrassment creeping up my neck.

Jiro's eyes twinkled with amusement as he looked up from the menu, catching me in my moment of uncertainty. "Having trouble, *koibito*?"

I let out a sheepish chuckle, feeling a bit like a fish out of water. "Just a little. The descriptions are quite elaborate."

He grinned, his voice a gentle melody. "Don't worry,

I've got this. How about I order for both of us?"

Relief washed over me, and I nodded gratefully. "That would be wonderful, thank you."

He winked playfully, his smile lighting up his face. "Consider it a chance for me to impress you outside the bedroom."

I playfully rolled my eyes, trying to hide my growing excitement. "You've already done enough of that, believe me."

Our waiter returned to take our orders, and Jiro's fluency in French was again impressive. As the waiter left, Jiro leaned back in his chair, his eyes never leaving mine.

"I have to admit, I wanted to impress you tonight. Show you that there's more to me than the dark, brooding persona you often see."

I met his gaze, my heart fluttering at the honesty in his words. "Jiro, you don't need to impress me. I've always known there's more to you than meets the eye."

Genuine surprise flickered across his features. "You have?"

I nodded, feeling a connection that ran deeper than words. "From the moment we met, I saw someone who's fiercely protective, someone who's willing to sacrifice for the people he cares about, even if he doesn't always show it."

He leaned in, his gaze unwavering. "And what else did you see?"

My heart raced, and I decided to speak from my heart. "I saw a man with layers, someone who's struggled and fought his way through life but who still has a capacity for tenderness and care."

His expression softened, and his thumb traced gentle circles on the back of my hand. "Hope, you have a way of seeing through me."

I laughed softly, feeling a warmth spread through me. "Maybe because I've always wanted to."

The air between us seemed charged, the connection deepening with each passing moment.

"Well, if my bedroom performance last night wasn't enough to impress you for a lifetime, I'll have to step up my game."

His words, though unexpected, made me burst into laughter, drawing curious glances from nearby tables.

My cheeks turned a shade of pink, and I couldn't help but play along. "Oh, I think you've already made quite the impression."

His laughter danced in the air, a melodious sound that blended seamlessly with the restaurant's sophisticated ambience. He gazed at me, his eyes intense with a hint of vulnerability I suspected he rarely showed. "And you, Hope Myers, have shown me a side of myself I never thought I'd find."

I wanted to keep the conversation light, but there were a lot of things I needed to know pertaining to my brother but also his intentions for afterward. I wanted to keep on dreaming. Of course I did. I wanted to keep on deluding myself that Jiro Saito was mine not only temporarily but forever.

As the waitress set the plate of *Chèvre chaud* in front of me, I could not ignore the more serious concerns we needed to address. Ones that I knew I couldn't ignore, no matter how much I wanted to remain wrapped in this beautiful dream. I let out a sigh, my mood dipping a little.

"Warm goat cheese salad," he translated with a smile. "Is that a problem?"

I chuckled, shaking my head. "Oh no! I love cheese." I picked up my cutlery. "I can't wait to try this."

Jiro noticed, and his brows furrowed slightly. "Why the sigh?"

I hesitated, my gaze dropping to my plate momentarily before I looked back at him. "I know I've been trying to keep the mood light tonight, and I want to, I really do. But there are things we can't avoid forever."

He nodded, his expression serious now. "I know."

I toyed with the greens on my plate, gathering my thoughts. "Maybe we should just let it go, you know. My brother is obviously alive, and if he doesn't care about his family, then why should I?"

He regarded me quietly for a moment before speaking. "Because you're not like that, Hope. You care deeply about everything and everyone. And if, by a sinister turn of events, he ends up dead because we didn't do anything, you would feel guilty. I can't stand the thought of you feeling the kind of guilt that's been haunting me for years."

His words touched a raw nerve, the truth behind them cutting deep. I couldn't help but feel a pang of bitterness. Jiro could never be mine; this pseudo-relationship could never be real until he stopped carrying Anna's death on his shoulders like that.

I nodded, my fingers tracing the rim of my wineglass.

"Hope, look at me."

I looked up and met his troubled eyes.

"It's not that simple anyway. It's not about your brother's potential fate. I won't lie; I don't care if Leo lives or dies. It's all about protecting you."

My heart clenched at his words. "Protecting me from what?"

He hesitated for a moment, his jaw tensing. "From Leo. From Valdez. I fear that your brother might do something else, something that could turn you into collateral, and that's something I can't stomach."

A shiver ran down my spine, the reality of his words sinking in. I understood the gravity of the situation, the danger that lingered around us. But at the same time, I couldn't shake the feeling that his need to protect me would always be a barrier between us.

He reached across the table, his hand gently covering mine. "I've called Hoka. He'll come here to help when Valdez makes contact. We'll make sure you're safe before I leave."

I managed a weak smile, trying to hide the pain my realization caused. My fingers trembled slightly beneath his touch. "Thank you. But what about you? Do you miss your friend, your life from before all of this?"

His gaze turned distant for a moment as if he was reminiscing. "Hoka was more than a boss to me. He's my best friend, my brother. And being an executioner is all I've ever known, so it's difficult to find my place once more." He looked back at me, his eyes burning with intensity. "Once all of this is over, once you're safe, I'll… I'll leave.

I'll continue to atone for my sins and try to find where I belong."

His words struck me like a blow, the realization that he would leave, that he saw himself as unworthy of anything beyond atonement. I fought to keep my voice steady, my emotions hidden. "And what about…?" I stopped talking, shaking my head.

He reached out, his thumb brushing against my cheek. "What about what?"

Tears welled up in my eyes, threatening to spill over. I took a deep breath, my voice shaking only slightly. "Nothing, let's eat."

The atmosphere at the table had shifted, the lightness and flirtation we had shared earlier replaced by a palpable tension that neither of us could ignore. I picked at my dessert, each bite of the beautifully presented dish tasting like a bittersweet reminder of the evening's unraveling.

Jiro's concern, as always, was evident in the furrow of his brow and the softness of his voice. "Is everything alright?"

I managed a nod, though the smile I forced felt fragile, almost like it could shatter at any moment. "Yes, this meal was delicious. Thank you so much for this amazing evening."

His frown deepened, and I could sense his unease. "I thought that maybe we could continue our evening after dinner." His hand moved to rub at his neck, a gesture that revealed his nervousness.

I understood his implication, the desire in his eyes mirroring my own. More than anything, I wanted to let the evening continue in the direction it had started, to lose myself in his arms and the pleasure he was bound to give me. But the reality of our situation was a heavy weight on my heart. I couldn't ignore the fact that we were nearing a goodbye, and I didn't know if my heart could handle getting lost in him more than I already was.

Shaking my head, my gaze locked with his, my voice coming out softer than I intended. "No, I'm sorry. I need to get home. My mom."

He nodded, a small smile playing on his lips, though it didn't quite reach his eyes. "Of course. Your mother comes first."

My heart ached at the finality of his words, the unspoken understanding that our time was running out. I managed a nod, my fingers gripping the edge of the tablecloth as if trying to hold on to something that was slipping away.

The drive back to my place was a quiet one, the air inside the car heavy with unspoken words and the weight of what our evening should have been. My gaze drifted out the window, the passing lights creating a blur of colors that matched the blur of my thoughts. I stole glances at Jiro from time to time, his profile illuminated by the soft glow of the dashboard lights, his expression something I couldn't quite decipher.

As we finally parked in front of my building, Jiro's voice broke the silence. "I'll call you as soon as Valdez makes contact."

I nodded, my throat tightening with emotions that threatened to spill over. I knew this was coming, that our time together was running out, but that knowledge didn't make the impending goodbye any easier. I turned to face him, my eyes holding his, silently conveying the ache in my heart.

He leaned in, his lips brushing against mine in a soft, lingering kiss that held a world of unspoken emotions. Pulling away, he whispered something in Japanese, his voice a soothing caress against my skin.

This time, I didn't ask what he had said. Somehow, I knew it was something precious, something that belonged to the intimacy of the moment and that whatever the meaning, it would probably break my heart.

I simply nodded, my heart heavy as I opened the car door and stepped out.

The night air felt cool against my skin as I walked toward the entrance of the building. As soon as the heavy door of the hall closed behind me, I leaned against it and let the melancholy wash over me.

I touched my lips, still feeling the ghost of his kiss, and closed my eyes. My heart ached, but I knew that no matter how painful, I had to let him go. I'd prayed for a savior, for a miracle, and I had received it in more than one way.

This savior in dark armor had come into my life like a tempest, leaving meforever changed.

***

The last two days had felt like an eternity without Jiro. No matter how much I tried to lie to myself, deny it, or distract myself, his absence was a constant ache in my chest. I missed him more than I thought possible; his presence was like a drug I was addicted to.

Oda had been texting me daily, trying to keep my

spirits up with his quirky jokes and overinflated ego. It was working to some extent. He had a way of making me laugh even when I didn't feel like it. But deep down, I knew he was also playing the role of intermediary between Jiro and me, relaying messages back and forth.

After finishing my shift at the emporium, I went to the bus stop, waiting to catch the bus to the weekly bingo game I hosted at the center. The afternoon sun was warm against my skin, but it did little to chase away the gloomy thoughts that had settled over me.

Just as I was lost in my own world, my phone rang, and I looked down to see Oda's name on the screen.

"Hey there," his voice greeted me, playfully teasing. "I was just hoping you're less sullen than the yakuza who's been moping in his bedroom for the past two days."

His words immediately made me chuckle as a feeling of warmth settled in my chest at the realization that Jiro was missing me, too. "Oh, you mean he's not having a grand time without me?"

Oda's laughter echoed through the line. "I think his sulking has reached epic proportions. So, how about we go grab some coffee? My treat."

Coffee sounded like a great idea, and spending time with Oda was always entertaining. "Sure, that sounds nice. But I have bingo in a bit, so it will have to be after that. Does that work?"

"Perfect, anything to get out of this pity party of one."

I was about to respond when I heard distant rumbling on the other end of the line. It seemed like a muffled conversation was taking place, and I could sense tension in the air.

"What? It's true. You're like an emo kid at his first My Chemical Romance concert." Oda's voice shot back, followed by some indistinct rambling.

"Ouch. Stop hitting me, man, fuck!" Oda suddenly snapped, the commotion on his end growing more chaotic. "Got to go, beautiful. I'll meet you at that little café you like in about two hours? Ouch, stop it!"

The prospect of seeing Oda was pleasant, but no matter how petty and childish it was, knowing that Jiro was miserable without me somehow made my heart do a little dance.

When I arrived at the community center, the secretary at the main entrance halted me with unexpected news. "Hope, the admin team is looking for you. They want to see you on the fourth floor."

Anxiety knotted in my stomach, instantly replacing any thoughts of Jiro with a growing sense of unease. As I rode the elevator to the fourth floor, my mind spun through potential scenarios, each one suggesting that my time might no longer be enough and that the price of my mother's care was about to increase.

The admin office door was ajar, and I hesitated for a moment before stepping in, taking a deep breath to try and calm my nerves.

When I pushed the door, my heart raced despite my attempt to calm myself.

Jenny, a middle-aged woman with vibrant red hair, greeted me with a cheerful smile as I entered her office. "Ah, there you are, Hope!" Her cheerful tone immediately eased some of my stress. Maybe this wouldn't be bad news after all.

"You wanted to see me?" I asked, my nerves still fluttering.

"Yes, I did. I wanted to discuss your mother's arrangement with us," she said, glancing down at the folder in front of her.

I nodded, trying to wrap my head around the situation. "Okay?"

Her smile remained, and she continued. "Well, we received an advance payment for three years of full-time care for your mother yesterday. I'm just wondering if you have a date in mind for when she would be moving in permanently. The room has been held, but we can't keep it reserved indefinitely."

I blinked, shocked by what she'd just said. An advance payment for three years of care? I certainly hadn't made any such arrangement. Suddenly, realization dawned on me, bringing a mixture of shock and hurt. Jiro. He must have been the one to make this payment to ensure that my mother was taken care of for years to come. But instead of feeling gratitude, a pang of hurt twisted within me. I stood there feeling like a charity case, and it stung.

I managed to gather my thoughts, my voice steady, but my heart conflicted. "I'll give you a date before the end of the week," I finally said, my mind racing as I tried to process everything.

"Thank you, Hope."

As I left the admin office, emotions churned within me like a stormy sea. Gratitude for Jiro's gesture tangled with a sense of shame, as if my circumstances had led him to make such grand decisions.

My initial plan of hosting bingo became a distant thought, overshadowed by this news. I hurried to the reception to explain that I had an emergency and wouldn't be able to lead the session today.

Outside the center, fresh air did little to quell the whirlwind of feelings inside me. Pulling out my phone, my fingers trembled as I dialed Jiro's number.

"I was not moping," he said on the other end, his tone bristling with frustration.

I was well beyond being even a little interested in his stupid banter with Oda. "Did you pay for three years of care for my mother?" The line fell silent, the pause only fueling my anger. "Do you have any idea how that makes me feel?"

"What?" His response held an edge, a coldness that made my steps falter.

"To know that everything between us, every gesture you make, comes from pity and misplaced guilt," I blurted out, my frustration overflowing.

"Everything?" he echoed, his voice taking on a chilling tone that caught me off guard. "Is that truly what you believe?"

Looking heavenward, I tried to find the right words. "It certainly feels that way."

"I see," he finally said, his voice softer but somehow scarier. "I'm not sure if there's anything I can say over the phone to change your perception. Goodbye, Hope."

The line went dead, leaving me standing there, emotions roiling within me. The situation between us just got even worse, and this time, I might be the one to blame.

With time to spare before meeting Oda, I decided to rein in my nerves. I refused to be that person who spends a coffee date with a friend whining about her... well, what was Jiro to me anyway? I couldn't help but snort at my own confusion. Jiro wasn't anything to me. Not really.

As I walked along the pier, I allowed the soothing scent of the sea and the gentle rhythm of the waves to work their magic on my tumultuous emotions. The whole situation with my mother's care was now much clearer. It was undoubtedly the best choice for both of us. But as I gazed out at the expansive sea, my mind began to wander into uncharted territories. What would not having to bear the full weight of my mother's care mean for my future? Could I finally go back to school, resurrecting the dreams I'd set aside when life had taken a difficult turn? The possibilities seemed both exhilarating and daunting. Could I start my life back where I had left it before the avalanche of responsibilities had come crashing down? The idea filled me with excitement, a feeling I hadn't experienced in a long while.

Lost in my thoughts of newfound potential, I continued my leisurely stroll along the pier. I imagined what it would be like to have a fresh start, to be able to take the reins of my life once more.

Eventually, I arrived at the café. Pushing open the door, I was fully expecting to see Oda sitting there with his usual cheerful smile. But as I walked in, my heart leaped into my throat. It wasn't Oda sitting there. It was Jiro. His expression was etched with fury, his dark eyes practically smoldering with anger.

Fuck, this one was going to hurt.

FOURTEEN

Jiro

Fuck, she's beautiful. That was my first thought when she stepped into the café. Her hair caught the light in a way that made it look like a cascade of golden lilac, and her blue eyes held depths of emotion that I knew I had no right to read.

I leaned back, my irritation growing. But even in the midst of my annoyance, I couldn't deny the magnetic pull she had on me. She turned her gaze toward me, and I watched as her smile, so warm and genuine, faded, replaced with uncertainty and apprehension.

How could she think that everything I did was driven by pity? There was no pity in the way I looked at Hope, in the way I wanted her, in the way I saw a fierce warrior spirit beneath her delicate exterior. She was as far from a damsel in distress as one could be.

It certainly wasn't pity that drove me to kneel in front of her, to explore her body with a hunger that bordered on desperation. Pity was nowhere in the equation when I found myself lost in the pleasures she ignited within me.

She swallowed, her posture shifting as she approached me. There she was, my beautiful warrior, caught in the cross fire of our tangled emotions.

"Where's Oda?" Her voice was like a sharp needle piercing the air between us, breaking through the charged silence.

"Otherwise occupied," I replied curtly, my gaze fixed on her. The truth was far from that simple, though.

Locked in the bathroom of my hotel room, to be precise. It was his fault, really. After their call, I had explicitly told him not to show up for his coffee date with Hope. But the fool had defied me, asserting his independence. He had a streak of stubbornness that was infuriating, and now he would deal with the consequences.

"I didn't expect to see you here."

"Clearly," I muttered in response, unable to keep the

bitterness out of my tone. I was pretty sure she would not have come if she'd known.

She took a seat across from me, and the atmosphere seemed to thicken with tension. "Is everything alright?" Her question was laced with genuine concern, but it grated on my nerves.

"Is everything alright?" I repeated, my voice dripping with sarcasm. "Well, I must say, Hope, I've had better days."

I watched her squirm in her seat, her discomfort evident. She seemed to struggle with her words as if grappling with something she wanted to say but couldn't quite articulate.

I leaned in slightly, my gaze locked onto hers, daring her to speak her mind.

"Look, I… I know you're upset about what I said on the phone," she finally started, her words tentative.

"Upset? Is that what you think I am? Upset?" My voice came out sharper than I intended, the frustration within me boiling over. It wasn't just about her words on the phone. It was about everything—the tangled mess we had become, the conflicting emotions that seemed to constantly swirl between us.

She looked down, swallowing visibly. Her next words were so soft that I almost missed them. "I didn't mean to sound ungrateful."

"Do you think that's what I'm upset about?" I shot back, my tone laced with exasperation. Her words were missing the mark, like trying to mend a deep wound with a Band-Aid.

"So you are upset!"

Her response sounded like an accusation. The tension in

the air was almost tangible, crackling between us like a live wire. I had half a mind to grab her face and kiss her until she couldn't remember her name.

I threw her a narrowed gaze. "Be ungrateful as much as you like. Be a little diva princess. Hell! You deserve to be! What bothered me is the low opinion you have of me."

Her eyes widened in shock, and I knew I had struck a nerve.

"Jiro, no. You—" She shook her head, her voice wavering with emotion. "I could never think badly of you! You're—have you seen to what length you went to help me?"

A bitter laugh escaped me before I could stop it. She didn't know I was the opposite of the knight in shining armor, and I wasn't even referring to my past as an executioner or my grim connection to her sister's death. No, it was the fact that I wanted her for myself, to relish her presence, her touch, and to desperately make her fall for me like I was falling for her, even when I had no right to claim her.

I was not a knight. I was a selfish bastard.

I leaned in, my gaze unwavering as it traced the contours of her face, resting momentarily on her inviting lips. "Tell me, *koibito*, do you believe, for even a moment, it was pity that drove me so deep into you that I could barely tell where you ended and where I began?"

Her face flushed, and an unexpected gasp escaped her as she noticed the waitress approaching to take her order. I leaned back in my seat, a smirk playing on my lips.

Hope glared at me, her lips pressed into a thin line.

She quickly gave her order to the blushing waitress,

who obviously heard everything I had said and turned toward me.

"Was all of this truly necessary?" Her tone was reprimanding, reminiscent of a strict teacher scolding a wayward student.

"I believe it was," I replied, my voice low, my dick twitching at her tone.

Hmmm, maybe that would be a game she and I could play one day… I shook my head. There could not be another time.

"Jiro, I—" Her words faltered, and I caught the shift in her gaze, her eyes moving past me toward the door. I frowned, curiosity getting the better of me. Her reaction changed to one of surprise, her eyes widening. My chest tightened at the sight, a sudden surge of jealousy rising within me.

I swiveled in my chair, almost unable to stop myself from reacting to whatever—or whoever—had caught her attention. My jaw clenched as my eyes landed on the newcomer, and the jealousy within me flared even hotter.

Fuck my life.

It was Hoka, dressed impeccably in a designer suit, his infant son strapped to his chest in a display of unmatched fatherly cool. But what set me off was the way Hope was looking at him—with a certain appreciation that I couldn't quite stomach.

The collective admiration of every woman in the café was practically palpable.

Hoka removed his aviator sunglasses, his gaze locking onto mine with a knowing glint in his eyes and a damn smirk playing on his lips. That smug bastard was definitely enjoying this situation.

"Do you know him?" Hope's voice was a soft whisper, carrying both curiosity and something else that grated on my nerves.

"I do," I muttered, my jaw tightening as Hoka made his way to the counter to order a drink. "It's a *married* man. And remember when I told you I'd be the only yakuza you'll ever have? I meant that," I added, my tone laced with irritation, throwing her a glare for emphasis.

A pink hue tinted her cheeks as she smiled, her eyes dancing with mischief. "If I didn't know better, I'd say you're jealous. And I believe you're not a yakuza anymore, are you?"

I grunted, my irritation turning into something that felt dangerously close to jealousy. "Keep testing me, Hope Myers, and you'll end up over my knees, butt naked, with my handprint across that tempting ass of yours."

She twisted on her seat, capturing her plump bottom lip between her teeth, and a jolt of desire shot through me. The way she looked at me, the challenge in her eyes—she wanted to push my buttons, to see how far she could take it.

My little vixen… Shit, she'd be the death of me.

Hoka walked over to us, his coffee in hand and a knowing glint in his eyes, and somehow I knew karma was going to hit me like a freight train for all the shit I gave him about his relationship with Violet, and I knew I deserved it.

"Jiro," he said with a nod before turning his attention toward Hope, a smile that was almost blinding forming on his lips. "Hope Myers…" he trailed off, his voice smooth like silk. "I've heard so much about you. I'm Hoka Nishimura. I'm sure Jiro must have shared a lot about me." He practically purred the words.

Oh, give me a fucking break!

Her reaction was like a train wreck I couldn't look away from. Wide-eyed and agape, she opened and closed her mouth like a fish out of water.

"Close your mouth, sweetheart," I snapped, my irritation obvious but also knowing that I was just adding fuel to Hoka's smugness. "You're drooling over a married father."

"I..." She blinked a few times, her face turning a shade of crimson. Irritation surged within me at her reaction. Her blushing was mine. "Yes, hi, sorry, sir. Hoka and baby. It's just... hello," she finished with a huff, clearly flustered.

I scowled at the table. Was this what I was reduced to? Maybe Oda was right—I was becoming the damn caveman he claimed I was.

Oda! I narrowed my eyes and looked back at Hoka, who just sat down.

"How did you find me?"

Hoka laughed, his eyes twinkling with amusement. "Nice to see you too after all this time. You look well."

I rolled my eyes. "Oda?" I ventured.

Hoka nodded, the grin on his face growing even wider. "Yes, I came to see you at your hotel, got a key card, and found our boy seething. You locked him in the bathroom."

I didn't even bother asking him how he managed to get a key to my room. But I could feel Hope's curious eyes on me, and it made the skin at the back of my neck prickle with embarrassment. I reached up to rub my neck, a reflexive response that only seemed to amuse Hoka even more, his grin bordering on triumphant.

"You locked him in the bathroom?" Hope's gasp pulled my attention back to her.

I shrugged, not willing to get into the details. "He wasn't listening," I mumbled, not sure whether I wanted to murder Hoka or Oda first.

The baby's cooing interrupted the tension, and he stretched his arms toward Hope, diverting everyone's attention to him—a welcome respite for me.

"What's your name, handsome?" Hope's voice was soft, her smile gentle as she extended a finger toward Yuko.

The baby cooed again, his tiny fingers grasping hers.

"Yuko," Hoka replied, his gaze never leaving her face. I could practically see the assessment happening, even if she appeared oblivious. Hoka Nishimura was sizing up my woman.

She's not your woman, Jiro. She deserves better. My conscience's reminder stung.

"He's so beautiful," Hope breathed, her fingers gently brushing against Yuko's cheek. Her excitement was palpable, and it was utterly endearing.

"Yes, he is," Hoka agreed, his pride evident. "Do you want to hold him?"

"Oh!" Hope's eyes lit up with awe and eagerness, her hands finding their way to her chest. She looked absolutely radiant. "Can I?"

Hoka nodded, skillfully loosening the straps that held Yuko. I wasn't sure if she fully grasped the significance of

Hoka's gesture. Allowing someone to hold his son, whom he cherished deeply, was not a trivial matter. It was bigger than even I could understand.

"Oh, who's the cutest boy in the whole world?!" Hope beamed, gently bouncing Yuko on her knees. At that moment, she was completely lost to the world, absorbed in the joy of playing with the heir of the yakuza.

"I wanted to show you a glimpse of what your future could be like," Hoka whispered, leaning toward me with a smirk that made my blood boil with want.

I sighed, frustration tugging at my composure. "Why are you even here, and why with the kid?" I directed my words at Hoka, though my gaze remained locked on Hope and Yuko.

"Violet wanted to come to Seattle with me, and she's getting a well-deserved spa break. Besides, it is my child, too," Hoka replied, a hint of defensiveness lacing his words. "We were two to make him, Jiro. Sharing the responsibilities equally is only fair."

I snorted, unable to fully conceal my skepticism. "Is that you talking or Violet? Because it sounds an awful lot like your wife."

Hoka's glare was swift and potent. "It doesn't make it any less true."

Shaking my head, I pushed my irritation aside. "You're wasting our time here. Valdez hasn't even reached out to me yet."

"No, but he called *me*."

My eyes narrowed; Valdez was a crafty bastard. "And what did he say?" I asked through gritted teeth.

Hoka shrugged, taking a sip of his coffee. "You know, the usual. He painted it as a friendly reminder of our shared past, and then he proceeded to *politely* ask that you stay away from business that supposedly has nothing to do with the yakuza." He sighed. "I told him that was not possible because you had a… *vested* interest in what could turn into collateral damage," he added, letting his eyes linger on Hope.

Hope's inquisitive glance in our direction didn't go unnoticed, and my frustration deepened.

"What else?"

Hoka looked directly at her, his expression unwavering. "He agreed to meet us on Saturday in a mutually agreeable location. He'll give me the details tomorrow." He turned toward Hope, "And you don't mind spending the day with my wife at the Four Seasons, do you? Violet can't wait to meet you."

Hope stopped bouncing Yuko and glanced at me with a questioning look. She was sharp, my woman. She knew that Hoka's offer wasn't just about hospitality—it was his way of ensuring her safety. I felt a spark of pride—she was seeking my approval before accepting Hoka's proposal.

I gave her a nod with a smile, feeling like a winner. She was seeking me out for reassurance, and that meant the world to me.

"How could I say no?" She started to bounce Yuko again. "It's very kind of you."

Our conversation continued for a few more minutes, covering trivial topics such as the hotel they were staying at and their plans for the next day, yet I knew that more pressing discussions awaited us.

Once Hoka was done with his coffee, he turned to Hope. "Hope, why don't you let my driver take you home? Jiro and I will take a walk. I want to show the pier to Yuko."

Hope pressed a kiss to Yuko's chubby cheek before handing him back to Hoka. "There's no need. I can take the bus."

Hoka's smile persisted. "No, please humor me. The driver is paid whether we use him or not."

She nodded and waited until Hoka secured Yuko on his chest once again. She seemed calm, but I knew her tells—the slight worry of her bottom lip and the rhythmic tapping of her foot.

I walked up to her side and lightly brushed my fingers on the back of her arm. "Everything will be fine," I assured her.

She nodded silently, and we walked out. The driver waiting by the car took a couple of steps toward us.

"Please, could you drive Miss Myers wherever she needs to go and come back to meet us at the end of the pier?"

The driver nodded and opened the back door, inviting Hope in.

As she walked toward the car, I couldn't help myself. Against all rational thought and my own best advice, I stepped forward, my heart pounding. Just as she was about to get into the car, I gently placed my hand on her arm, turning her to face me.

Her eyes widened in surprise, and before she could say anything, I leaned in and kissed her. It was soft and brief, yet it held all the intensity of my feelings for her. When I pulled away, her lips were slightly parted, and her cheeks were flushed. I saw all her emotions shining in her beautiful eyes—surprise, longing, and maybe a touch of apprehension.

"Be safe," I whispered.

She nodded, her voice caught in her throat. "You too, please."

I released her arm, allowing her to get into the car, and as it pulled away, I turned to find Hoka standing beside me, his expression thoughtful.

"I like her," Hoka said, his gaze fixed on the disappearing car. "She's strong, good. She reminds me a lot of Violet."

I nodded, my own gaze lingering on the spot where the car had vanished. "Yeah, she's something else."

Hoka turned to me with a knowing smile. "You're in deeper than you want to admit, aren't you?"

I sighed, running a hand through my hair. "You have no idea. But between her and me, it's just not feasible."

Hoka's shrug was casual, his attention shifting to his son Yuko, who was nestled comfortably against his chest. "He's living proof that it's possible."

I shook my head; I was not in the right headspace to have this conversation now. "Let's walk."

So we continued, the sound of our footsteps mingling with the faint whispers of the sea. Despite this serene atmosphere, I could not stop thinking of a subject that was haunting me far more than I initially anticipated—Hoka's recent trip to Japan. It was crucial to clear the air before Valdez's meeting; I couldn't afford distractions.

"Sometimes the past is just too heavy to build a future," I began, the words reflective of my inner turmoil.

Hoka's expression turned contemplative for a moment before he shook his head, his gaze fixed on the horizon. "Two years ago, I might have agreed with you. But not now. If intentions are pure and both parties are committed, a lot can be overcome. Look at what Violet and I managed to conquer."

The question I had been suppressing pushed its way out. "And what about us? Have we truly moved past our issues?"

Hoka's pace slowed as he frowned at me. "Of course. You know we have."

Have we? I thought a little bitterly. Taking a deep breath, I decided it was time to address the unease. "I thought you trusted me, even after I stepped down from being your *wakagashira*."

Hoka stopped in his tracks, pivoting to face me squarely. "Spit it out, Jiro, because you're not making much sense."

"Were you ever going to tell me about your trip to Japan with Alessandro?"

Hoka nodded, resuming our walk toward the pier's end, his pace unhurried. "Ah."

"Ah? That's all you'll say."

He chuckled softly. "I do have more to say. Oda is a little bitch for gossiping like a teenager, but I was going to tell you. I was!" he insisted when I threw him a suspicious look. "I wanted to avoid getting either of our hopes up."

"Hopes for what?" My frown deepened as genuine confusion clouded my expression.

Hoka halted just as we reached the pier's end, his gaze focused on the tranquil expanse of Elliott Bay. The waters seemed calm, like our conversation, as if it were a prelude to the storm that may come. Yuko's infectious giggles punctuated the air as he playfully reached out toward the swooping seagulls.

"I miss you, Jiro. Deeply. Life, the business…" Hoka's voice trailed off, a sigh underscoring his words. "You've been gone for nearly two years, and nothing feels quite the same without you."

My gaze shifted downward, focusing on the gray, weathered stones beneath my feet. Guilt and ghosts of my past mistakes pressed upon me, their presence a heavy weight. I had sacrificed myself to safeguard our clan from a brewing war, one that threatened to shatter Hoka's newfound family. Yet, in the recesses of my mind, I couldn't escape the realization that they wouldn't have been in this predicament in the first place if I hadn't intervened in Hoka's relationship with Violet.

"The dealings with the Italians are flourishing, to say the least. Our business in multiple regions has grown by almost forty percent," Hoka continued, his gaze holding mine. "The elders are overjoyed."

"Okay?" My confusion lingered, his words a puzzle I was struggling to decipher.

A sidelong smile played on his lips, acknowledging the evident perplexity in my voice. "It means the elders are feeling rather benevolent. In fact, Sandro and I shared with them the truth about what happened in the warehouse the day my uncle died."

"You didn't!" I exclaimed, a huff escaping me. Such a revelation could have easily turned disastrous. Alessandro, Violet's mobster brother, had executed Hoka's uncle to shield Violet. It was a reckless act, given Violet wasn't yet bound to Hoka. Such audacity, taking down a yakuza elite like that, could have started an all-out war. But I had stepped in, shouldering the blame. It was the least I could do after all the chaos I'd inadvertently caused between Hoka and Violet. They deserved peace, even if it meant I lost my position, my identity, in the process.

Hoka's smirk deepened. "Oh, I did," he affirmed, his eyes locked with mine. "Now, the question is—will you reclaim your position as my *wakagashira*? Return to the world we once ruled side by side?" The invitation, laden with past memories and a potential future, hung thick in the air between us.

For a few heartbeats, I stood frozen. I had been convinced that this future was an impossibility. I had been exiled, and despite the past two years teaching me to savor the taste of freedom, the recent weeks had reshaped me. Despite my ongoing self-inflicted torment over not fitting into Hope's life, I couldn't deny the allure of the prospect. A life entwined with hers danced before my mind, a vision I found both exhilarating and terrifying.

"Okay... that's not quite the reaction I anticipated," Hoka interjected, a perplexed furrow creasing his brows. His demeanor seemed slightly irked. "I thought you'd be eager to return."

"No, wait, yes, I am." My response was a tangled admission, a candid reflection of my own inner turmoil. "It's just that… this is so unexpected, and given everything—"

Hoka raised his eyebrows knowingly. "Ah," he nodded in understanding. "Everything. Well, remember, nothing prevents you from taking 'everything' along with you. The summer house is yours, spacious enough for a family if that's what you're considering."

A family with Hope… My gaze shifted involuntarily toward Yuko. The image unfolded vividly in my mind—a life where Hope and I were together, the two of us creating a baby of our own. Yet, amid that enticing vision, a fierce internal struggle raged. I had fought so ardently to free Hope from the burdens she had long carried, to liberate her from the weight of her past. Was it not hypocrisy to then potentially shackle her to a different kind of confinement, to deny her the chance to savor genuine freedom?

What kind of man would that make me?

The monster you're always claiming to be, the insidious voice taunted from within.

I looked down at Yuko, his restlessness growing evident.

"The little guy's probably hungry; the milk is in the bag in the car," Hoka chimed in casually, his tone lightening the mood.

"Too cool to carry it yourself?" I retorted with a laugh.

He snorted, a playful smile tugging at his lips. "Please, I'm cool enough to pull that off." His expression grew more serious. "Listen, just think about it, okay? We can revisit this discussion once the Valdez situation is behind us. Alright?"

I nodded in acknowledgment, and we turned back, heading toward the car parked in its familiar spot. "I'll swing by your hotel tomorrow. Maybe you should bring some food for Oda tonight. I'm sure he's still pissed off," Hoka offered as he got into the car.

"Tell you what, I'll get him a case of beer and a burger, and we'll call it even," I quipped, closing his car door before watching him drive away. Turning, I retraced my steps up the street to where my bike was parked.

My mind was a whirlwind. Yes, I was reclaiming my life, but it wasn't the same life. I had evolved, transformed by the woman who had altered my very existence.

The quiet whisper surfaced again, a gentle yet persistent suggestion. Maybe she'd want to come with you. Perhaps she didn't yearn for that form of freedom.

I sighed, shaking my head as I swung a leg over the bike's saddle. No, I couldn't presume her desires. I couldn't coerce her into a life she hadn't sampled, a choice she hadn't even been given the opportunity to consider.

It would be a twisted pact, a manipulation of sorts, and I couldn't permit myself to be that selfish.

Hope Myers mattered too much to me. I couldn't deny it any longer. And for her sake, I had two options—stay and transform into the man she deserved, or leave and ensure that I'd never return.

FIFTEEN

Hope

The soft hum of the ceiling fan overhead was the only sound in the room as I began packing up my mother's belongings. I looked at her, fast asleep in the single bed, as I moved silently around the room.

It was not all bad, though. I was pleased she was starting a new chapter in her life at the center, and she would have access to all the care she needed there.

Pausing for a moment, I sat on the edge of the bed, letting my thoughts drift to the unexpected encounter earlier today. Meeting Hoka at the café was not something I had anticipated, especially not with a baby cradled lovingly in his arms. The sight of the stern yakuza boss playing with his child was nothing short of surreal. I couldn't help but smile, thinking of the tender way he'd held the baby, the loving gaze he directed at the little one. It was a stark contrast to what one might imagine when thinking of a feared underworld figure.

I found myself wondering about Violet, his wife. Was she traditional or more like me, with dreams and ambitions that stretched beyond family roles? The eagerness and apprehension to meet her on Saturday bubbled inside me.

I toyed with the thin yellow scarf in my hand. The sight of Hoka and his baby made something stir within me. If the boss of the yakuza could find happiness, domesticity, and perhaps even normalcy in the midst of his tumultuous world, then why couldn't Jiro and I have that future?

He needs to want it, though, the voice in my head whispered, causing a pang of doubt.

The gentle vibration of my phone broke my concentration. Instinctively, I thought it might be Max again, asking if I could cover for him in the morning. I rolled my eyes in advance, preparing to send a half-joking, half-serious reply.

But when I grabbed my phone, my heart did a little flip.

It was Jiro.

Are you up?

My brows knitted in confusion as I walked out of the room and closed the door behind me. It was past midnight. I hadn't even realized how engrossed I'd become in my task, losing track of time. Why would he be texting at this hour?

Yes, packing my mother's stuff. Is everything okay? I replied, fingers hastily typing out the message.

His response came quickly, causing a fresh wave of anxiety and excitement. *Yes. I just want to see you. I'm in front of your building.*

The flurry in my stomach felt like I'd swallowed a herd of wild broncos, each one bucking and kicking with anticipation. Without thinking, I rushed to the window, peering down, half expecting to see him looking up. But of course, I couldn't make out any details from this height.

I hurried to the door, suddenly hyperaware of my appearance. My oversized white shirt had probably seen better days, my yoga pants were not the most flattering, and I could only imagine the state of my hair. But this was Jiro. The man always looked flawless, like he'd walked out of a fashion magazine. And when I opened the door, he didn't disappoint. There he was in dark blue jeans that fit him just right and a green Henley shirt that made his eyes pop. It wasn't fair, really.

"My mother is asleep," I whispered, not wanting to wake her. I motioned for him to follow me into the living room, moving aside some of the boxes to make space. "I'm packing her things for the center. I… Thank you for what you did. I shouldn't have reacted that way."

He exhaled softly, his eyes searching mine. "It's okay. I probably didn't handle things the best way either."

I shook my head, feeling that familiar warmth rush to my cheeks. "No, but your intentions were right. And that means everything."

Jiro's towering presence made my already modest apartment feel even smaller. He had a way of consuming space, not just with his size but with the energy he brought with him. It was intimidating and comforting all at once.

I took a deep breath, feeling the weight of worry press on my chest. "What's going on? Is it Leo? Is he dead?" I asked, my voice trembling slightly.

Jiro's expression softened, and he looked almost sheepish, a sight I wasn't accustomed to. "No, nothing happened to Leo," he said, shaking his head. "I know my timing isn't ideal, and midnight visits aren't exactly reassuring."

He then raised his hand, revealing a paper bag. "I just… I brought you chocolate," he said, a hint of humor in his eyes.

I blinked in surprise, trying to process this unexpected gesture. From deep concerns about Leo to… chocolate?

I chuckled softly, my nerves now mixed with amusement. "Chocolate, Jiro? At this hour?"

His lips quirked up in a teasing smile. "Thought you might appreciate a little midnight treat. Besides," he added, glancing at the moving boxes scattered around, "I remember promising you a full box once."

I opened the box, revealing the luxurious Godiva chocolates inside. Memories flooded back. "You remembered that day with Anna?" I asked, astonished. It was a fleeting moment from years ago when he'd gifted Anna a box, and I'd sneakily eaten a few. Anna had been livid.

His gaze softened, almost making my heart ache. "Every moment," he whispered.

"What is it?" I asked softly, resting the bag on the console and going to stand in front of him. "Is something wrong with you? Do you want to talk about it?"

He gave me a small smile and brushed his knuckles across my cheek before letting his hand fall to the side. "I couldn't sleep, and I kept on thinking, what are you going to do now? I mean, once we meet with Valdez."

"Oh." I chewed on my bottom lip, not really expecting the question, especially not at this time. I walked to the sofa and gestured for him to join me.

I sat down, waiting for him to do the same before continuing. "Is that what stopped you from sleeping? What will I do once it's over?"

He shrugged. "Partially."

Could he have been more cryptic?

I sighed. "Honestly, I don't know. It's all so up in the air right now, and not even a few weeks back, it felt like it would always be the same. Things just unraveled so quickly I didn't even have a chance to think about what my future would look like."

Except that I would have wanted it to be with you, I thought, but knew how desperate it would sound if I said it.

He watched me intently, waiting for more.

I leaned back in my seat. "I've been so tied down by

obligations, it felt like a safety net. But now, with everything changing, it's daunting. It's like you and your legacy. You were born into this life."

He winced slightly, and I immediately regretted my words. "Jiro, I didn't mean—"

He held up a hand, silencing me. "I know, it's all good, and I know only too well what you mean. Sometimes, having a set path feels freeing. Without it, the endless possibilities can be paralyzing."

I blinked, the weight of his words settling in my heart. The room was filled with a heavy silence, punctuated only by the distant hum of the city outside. His midnight appearance, the chocolate, and his probing about my dreams felt disjointed, yet there was an underlying intention that eluded me. It seemed he was searching, not necessarily for clear answers but for insights into my soul.

"I… I don't know," I admitted, my voice barely above a whisper. "I've always dreamed of taking art classes, maybe even opening a small studio. And a house by the sea, with a white picket fence, where I can wake up to the sound of waves every morning." I smiled wistfully, lost in the dream.

As I spoke, I noticed a fleeting shadow cross Jiro's face, a hint of disappointment or perhaps sadness. Before I could ask him about it, a voice from the other room broke our intimate bubble.

"Anna!" My mother's voice echoed, her tone urgent.

The moment shattered. Jiro stood up abruptly, his demeanor changing from vulnerable to guarded in an instant. "I should go," he said, his voice strained. "I've kept you up long enough."

"But, Jiro—" I began, but he placed a finger on my lips, silencing me.

He leaned down, his lips brushing the top of my head in a tender kiss. "Remember, Hope," he murmured, his voice thick with emotion, "no matter where life takes you, always chase the dreams that set your soul on fire."

And with that, he was gone, leaving me alone in the room with the lingering scent of his cologne and the weight of his words.

"You, Jiro Saito," I whispered to the empty room, my voice trembling with emotion, "you set my soul and world on fire." The words hung in the air, a silent testament to a love that was deep, raw, and undeniable. Every fiber of my being ached for him, yearning for the connection we shared.

I stared at the door he'd just closed, wishing he could hear my silent confession, hoping that someday, our souls would find their way back to each other.

Sixteen

Hope

Things were changing quickly, maybe a little too quickly, and I was not sure if I liked that or not. I'd dropped my mother at the center yesterday, and it felt weird to go back home alone, being able to remove all the protections and locks that used to be placed everywhere.

I had lain in my bed most of the night, staring at the dark ceiling, not really knowing what I would do with my life once things with my stupid brother were settled.

For the past few years, I'd been driven by my need to take care of my mother. My family. But what now? Now that she was set and cared for. Now was the time to look at me, and that was scary.

Who did I want to be? I was not the Hope that entered university, her head full of silly dreams. I could not just step back into the life I left three years ago; I didn't fit in this mold anymore.

I needed to figure out who I was now as Hope Myers, not as the carer but the woman, and the only thing I knew for sure was that I wanted to keep the only thing I couldn't have… Jiro.

At least, that was what I thought until I walked into the biggest suite of the Four Seasons hotel, escorted by two guards, to see Hoka's wife coming toward me with a wide smile on her face.

That woman was nothing I would have expected a Mafia wife to be. She was not dressed in some posh, high couture outfit but wore a pair of skinny jeans and an oversized one-shoulder red top that was so striking against her creamy white skin. She was probably just a few years older than me, with black hair in a messy bun and blue eyes that made me think of Snow White, and she was just a little ball of positive energy.

"Hope! I'm so happy to meet you!" She beamed, pulling me into a hug before I even had the chance to answer. "Yuko is asleep! Come, I had some food brought up for us." She grabbed my hand and led me into the room. "I want to know everything about you." Her enthusiasm was infectious, and I couldn't help but laugh along.

We settled in her living area, and she sat across from me, her excitement palpable.

"Please, help yourself." She pointed at the cart, which was loaded with way more food than both of us could eat.

She seemed to catch my thoughts and wrinkled her nose. "I might have gone a little overboard, huh?" She sighed, waving her hand dismissively. "I didn't know what you liked, so…"

Her consideration immediately put me at ease and filled me with gratitude. She genuinely wanted me to feel comfortable with her, and that meant a lot to me.

"What's on your mind?" Her sidelong smile made me realize I'd been staring at her.

I blushed and looked down at the fine china plate adorned with blue flowers in front of me. "Oh, nothing."

"You're surprised that I'm Hoka's wife," she said with certainty.

I looked up with wide eyes. Was I that transparent? Did I offend her? Oh God, she's going to hate me now. "I—"

She laughed and waved her hand in a dismissive gesture. "Oh no, don't look so pitiful! It's such a legitimate thought. Hell! We've been together for years. We have a beautiful boy, and sometimes I still wonder how it works."

I mustered a smile that probably resembled a grimace, and she chuckled again.

She began to fill her plate with food, and I followed suit

as she continued talking. "Honestly, I know on paper, Hoka and I could not be more incompatible. Some people thought and prayed we would fail." She shrugged, taking a bite of a mini sandwich, which made me laugh once more.

"It's just that… I'm not sure what I was expecting." I admitted, a bit shy.

"You probably expected a proper and rigid Asian lady in her thirties, all bound by conventions." She snorted. "Hoka would have been miserable if he'd married her. We had a rough journey, more than rough if I'm being honest with you. There was a long time when I thought we were all wrong for each other, and he thought he was all wrong for me. But looking back, that's exactly why we needed each other. Being too similar is just boring. Hoka completes me just like I complete him."

As she spoke, the air in the room seemed to grow heavy with unspoken emotions. Her words echoed in my mind, and the similarity between her situation and mine struck me hard. But they had fought for their love, faced challenges and differences, and come out stronger on the other side.

"Hope, is something bothering you?" Violet leaned in, her brow furrowing as she studied my face for any sign of distress.

I shifted uncomfortably in my seat, my heart feeling like a battlefield. I took a deep breath, then blurted out, "What if you love someone, but they keep pushing you away?"

Violet's eyes softened, and she leaned in slightly. "Love is a complex thing, especially in the world Hoka and Jiro come from. Sometimes people push others away not because they don't care, but because they care too much."

I swallowed hard, feeling tears prick at the corners of my eyes. "What if they're leaving to protect you?"

Violet's gaze held mine, and she sighed softly. "Hoka told me not to meddle, but I can't help myself. When someone wants to leave you, it could be their way of showing love, misguided as it might be. They might believe that it's the best thing for you, even if it breaks their own heart."

A tear slipped down my cheek, and I hastily wiped it away. I would not embarrass myself in front of a woman I'd just met.

Violet's voice lowered, carrying a touch of sadness. "Leaving behind your *koi no yokan* is one of the hardest things. It's a Japanese term for the feeling you have when you first meet someone and know that, someday, you will love them. It's like a premonition of love. But sometimes, life has its own plans, even when we're not ready to accept them."

I was startled by the unfamiliar term, my curiosity piqued. "*Koi no yokan*?"

Violet seemed a bit embarrassed by her slip, but she smiled gently. "It's a concept that's quite personal. Hoka believes that you and Jiro are soul mates. Based on Jiro's actions, he's convinced of it. That's probably why he's trying to protect you in his own, albeit misguided, way."

My heart ached at Violet's words. Soul mates? It sounded like something out of a fairy tale. "But he's going to leave, he told me. How can that be love?"

Violet reached out and touched my hand, her eyes filled with understanding. "Sometimes, people believe that by leaving, they're giving the greatest gift. They might think they're sparing you from pain or danger. It's a twisted way of loving, but it's still love."

"I don't want that."

"No, I didn't think you would." She gave my hand a reassuring squeeze before letting go. "That man is laden with emotional scars, just like my Hoka. And…" She made a rueful face. "Jiro and I didn't exactly start on the best footing, but one thing I know is that he's highly honorable and incredibly stubborn. Now he's returning as Hoka's *wakagashira*."

"Is that so?" I tried to sound nonchalant, but the idea both pleased and saddened me. I knew how much he missed his previous life. Of course, he would return to it.

She sighed. "He hadn't told you, had he?" She caught her bottom lip between her teeth before letting it go with a sigh. "I'm really making a mess of things, aren't I?" she muttered under her breath. "Hoka told me to leave it alone, but I think I helped with Alessandro and Lily, I thought…" She shook her head and stuffed another small sandwich in her mouth.

I couldn't help but smile; this woman was so much more like me than I could have ever comprehended. I also had the gift to put my foot where I shouldn't.

"He probably would have told me, but I was busy yesterday taking my mother to the center and all." I shrugged; he probably waited for this mess to be settled before telling me. Not that he owed me an explanation. We're not together or anything. He didn't make a commitment.

Lord knows I didn't need that to be completely addicted

to the man.

Violet looked at me silently as she drank her hot chocolate.

"Not that I don't appreciate his help and your husband's help with my brother's mess," I added quickly, hoping she didn't misunderstand my words and thought I was ungrateful.

She smiled, and it looked like it carried so many secrets. "You know my husband, he's not perfect. He's a loving husband and doting father, but outside of our bubble, he's as ruthless as they come, you know? He's not very charitable. He doesn't just help people for the sake of helping them."

"Okay…" I was not sure where she was going with that.

Her smile widened. "What I'm trying to say is that Hoka is helping because Jiro is family and because you're not just anyone. You've probably already noticed that Jiro can be quite stubborn and too caught up in his own self-blame to hear reason."

I snorted, and she chuckled. "He asked Hoka for help," she continued, looking at me expectantly as if I should catch on to what she was hinting at.

"I know, and I really appreciate it," I replied.

She rolled her eyes. "No, Hope, you're not getting it. Jiro Saito asked Hoka for help to protect *you*. I don't care about what he says or doesn't say, and subtlety be damned. Jiro loves you, whether he's aware of it or not."

This revelation caught me off guard, my heart racing wildly in my chest. Jiro loving me? Could that even be possible? I was well aware he cared for me, sure, but he had never reciprocated when I confessed my love to him during our most intimate moments.

I think Violet had left out a crucial variable in her equation—the immense guilt that Jiro felt for my sister's death and the overwhelming sense of debt he believed he owed.

"My sister died twelve years ago," I disclosed, trying to keep my voice steady despite the emotional weight of the memory.

Violet's expression turned somber. "I know."

I took a deep breath, steadying myself. "I was barely ten back then, and Anna was looking after me for the day on campus when I saw Jiro for the first time. He came to see her on campus as a surprise. They'd only been seeing each other for a few weeks then. I had an instant crush on him and did my best to be around whenever he was there. I was a little stalker," I admitted with a humorless chuckle. "Of course, I was too young to understand what was happening. My sister started receiving threatening notes, and Jiro was worked up, saying it might be the yakuza unhappy about his involvement with an outsider." I shrugged. "I didn't grasp the gravity of it—yakuza, threats—it was all beyond me. All I cared about was that beautiful man I was convinced I'd marry someday." I shook my head at my naive younger self.

Violet listened attentively, her calm presence making it easier to share one of my most painful memories.

"I wasn't even supposed to be there that day. Leo was angry with Anna—he always was those days—and he took me to her place to disrupt her date with Jiro. He dropped me off at the bottom of her building, and when I got up there, the door was open. Jiro and Anna were arguing. I don't know what it was about, but he stormed out, and she followed him. I don't think she even saw me standing there, and that was the last time I saw her alive."

Violet nodded solemnly. "I'm sorry, losing someone we care about is so hard," she offered, her tone carrying her own pain. She truly understood.

"Jiro is tormented by guilt over her death," I added.

She nodded again. "Yes, he is."

This simple acknowledgment should have brought some relief, but instead, it stung.

"But Jiro doesn't function like that. I've seen how he acts around Hoka and me. If anything, his guilt isn't what pulls him closer; it's what's pushing him away. Jiro is a man who would walk away from his own happiness because of his guilt."

I sighed, my heart heavy with the weight of these revelations. "With Jiro, it's just that…"

Yuko's noises filtered through the baby monitor. "Ah, the little man is up," Violet said, standing up. "Hold that thought. I'll be right back."

I nodded, using this moment to check my phone. There were messages from my brother urging me to meet them in the hotel hallway.

I stood up from my seat, leaving my bag on the table to show Violet that I was going to return in a minute, and informed the scary-looking guard that I'd be back in just a moment and that I just needed to go to the hotel boutique for some women issues. I knew it was something that nobody would ever question, and he nodded, clearing his throat.

As soon as I reached the lobby, I was pulled into a

meeting room. I turned around and found my brother pacing back and forth. His appearance was disheveled, his hair mussed, and his eyes carried a wild edge I'd not seen since Anna's death.

He wasted no time; his words spilled out like a torrent, fueled by both panic and anger. "I told you to walk away, Hope, I told you to stay away from that fucking yakuza. It's everything you did that led to this mess. It's all on your head!" He pointed an accusatory finger at me, his voice trembling with frustration.

His accusations struck me like a punch to the gut, causing anger to bubble inside me. "Hold on a minute! You think I asked for any of this? You think I wanted any of these troubles? You disappeared, Leo! You left us in the deep shit you created. How did you even know I was here?"

He paced back and forth erratically, his hands gesturing wildly. "You had choices, Hope. You always had choices, and you chose to sleep with him just like Anna!" he barked, ignoring my question.

My patience began to fray, my frustration mingling with a growing suspicion. "What are you not telling me, Leo? Why are you so vehement about all this? What are you hiding?"

He seemed to waver but looked away, his hands trembling. "Nothing good comes from digging into the past. You kept pushing deeper into it when I asked, no, demanded that you stop. But his dick was too good to pass up, huh?"

My patience snapped, replaced by raw irritation. "What does it have to do with you? You left! I thought you were dead, and you know what? For the first time, I wished you might have been!" I turned back toward the door. "I have someplace to go."

He stepped closer, his expression filled with desperation and bitterness. "What happens next, Hope, is on your head. Remember that."

I was done with him, with his drama. I didn't care what happened to him now. I opened my mouth to tell him that, but before I even got a chance to turn around, a cloth was pressed against my face from behind. Panic surged, but before I could react, darkness overtook me, and everything went black.

SEVENTEEN

Jiro

After spending several hours with the local yakuza to ensure we had the manpower we needed and briefing their leader about the potential fallout from our cartel meeting, Hoka and I were en route to meet Valdez.

"Have you decided yet?" Hoka asked, his gaze focused on the road as the car glided through the city's streets.

"Decided what?" With everything going on, I wasn't sure which decision he was referring to.

Hoka cast a sideways glance at me. I sensed he wanted to know if I'd return as his *wakagashira*. The decision should've been easy. Of course, I wanted to return. But then there was the girl I kept insisting I'd leave behind. Whenever I considered my old life, she became a dominant thought, seemingly integral to any decision.

"What I don't get," Oda chimed in from the front seat, "is how you can say you're protecting Hope from Valdez, yet you're not fully committed…" His tone dripped with sarcasm.

Suppressing a grin, Hoka looked down at his lap, reminding me of our earlier disagreement. Oda continued, "I mean, if it helps, I can claim her. I'm sure Hope and I would get along—"

Reacting instantly, I slapped the back of his head.

"Ow! Seriously?"

"I'll do it again until you grow up, kid!"

"I'm twenty-four!"

"You sure don't act it," I shot back as the car stopped outside a row of commercial buildings.

"Ready?" Hoka adjusted his jacket and checked his gun.

"Is meeting him here really a good idea?" The reflective windows of the building gave me a sense of unease.

Hoka tried to sound confident. "Valdez isn't foolish enough to start a war. As long as we hold up our end, we're fine." But we both knew my real concern.

As we exited the car, Hoka straightened his suit. "If things go south, it might force you to decide."

I smirked. "Oh, how appealing."

His grin was wry. "Sure, I bet you'd hate having Hope in your bed every night. Tough luck, Jiro."

Before I could reply, Hoka's phone pinged. One of Valdez's men beckoned us. As Hoka read the message, he hesitated. A sense of dread consumed me, taking me back to a tragic memory two years ago. I now had a better understanding of Hoka's distress from back then. And for that, I owed him an apology.

"Hope…" I whispered, seeing her in a chair, handcuffed and slumped, unconscious.

My fingers instinctively reached for the gun in my holster. To hell with peace. Valdez was seconds away from a bullet.

Valdez quickly raised his hands, attempting a calming gesture. "Calm down. She's unharmed. We can talk like reasonable men, and she'll be safe."

"You took her from the hotel where she was with *my wife*, under *my protection*?" Hoka's voice was steel, his yakuza leader persona emerging.

Valdez's bravado wavered. "I didn't mean any offense. I asked her brother to bring her. I needed to prove he wouldn't sell out his family *again*." Valdez's gaze shifted to the side, his lips twisted in disgust. "I was wrong."

Following his gaze, I saw Leo Myers. My contempt for the man deepened—he was even worse than I'd feared. My fingers itched to shoot him. But my attention shifted back to Hope, her vulnerability diming my anger.

"I need to make sure she's okay before we continue," I said, my voice tight.

Valdez's smile was devoid of mirth as he nodded toward Hope. "Go ahead."

I signaled for Oda to check on Hope, wanting to keep my eyes on Valdez and her treacherous brother. She stirred as Oda cupped her face, her wide eyes reflecting her fear. The thought of her brother causing her more pain incited a rush of anger, fueling my urge to physically retaliate.

Oda whispered to her, and she quieted, her distress easing. I clenched my teeth, realizing I should be the one calming her, not delegating that role.

Despair sank in. Would I be capable of providing the emotional support she needed? Despite Oda's reassurances, her gaze darted to me, and I could see trust and wonder in her eyes.

I managed a small smile, hoping to alleviate some of the jealousy that had been churning within me. She sought me, always me.

Then she looked toward her brother, and the intensity in her eyes was lethal. I couldn't help but grin. *That's my girl.*

Hoka's tone was biting. "You promised civility. This isn't it."

"Neither is the yakuza meddling in our business," Valdez snapped back.

"Hope has a connection to me," I blurted out instinctively, my words ringing louder than I intended.

Valdez raised an intrigued eyebrow. "Really? Because my man Pedro tells me you never mentioned her before."

"Well, I'm mentioning her *now*." I was leaning into the

role of a possessive alpha male, which wasn't too far from the truth. I glanced at her, and, unsurprisingly, her glare was squarely on me. She certainly disliked this display.

"So you're claiming her as yours?"

I hesitated briefly, contemplating the ramifications of a "yes" answer. I didn't want to control her choices, as an official claim would demand, yet at this moment, it seemed essential to establish my position. But before the words escaped, I was surprised to hear myself saying, "Yes."

Valdez acknowledged my response with a nod. "Very well. In the spirit of our collaboration, I'll pledge that you're safe from us. But I also ask that you stop sniffing into our business."

Hoka's nod was sharp and decisive. "Yakuza have no interest in your business, Valdez. Our primary concern was ensuring Hope's safety and satisfying her inquiries."

Valdez shifted his focus. "Is Hope Myers the sole individual you're claiming?"

I understood his unspoken query—was Leo Myers also under my protection? Before I could respond, Hoka intervened, his tone carrying a fierce edge. "Yes, she's the only one."

"Alright then." Valdez gestured toward Hope. "Take the girl and go."

With that motion, my world shifted. There it was, the tattoo that had haunted my nightmares for over a decade. It was the bizarre image of a snake entwined around an eagle's talons, the serpent biting into the bird. It felt surreal, like a figment of my imagination. Memories of an alley flooded back, and my hand instinctively reached for my gun, pointing it at Valdez's head.

"Jiro…" Hoka's voice rang with an unfamiliar caution.

I cocked the gun, the metallic sound cutting through the tense air, accompanied by a symphony of other guns being readied—Valdez's men, most likely, preparing to aim at me. Yet, I was heedless of their presence.

"Jiro!" Hoka's tone sharpened, his command aimed squarely at me. "Lower your weapon, now!"

My hand trembled, my finger twitching near the trigger. The burning hatred and vengeance ignited a fire within me that made it difficult to breathe.

"He struck first, Hoka. He tried to end me," I spat, the words sharp and accusing. The memories of that alley resurfaced, mingling with the searing pain of Anna's loss. "I have every right to take his life."

"What are you talking about? I'd never be stupid enough to cross a yakuza," Valdez countered, raising his hands in a slow, deliberate gesture. Around the room, I heard the distinct sound of guns being uncocked, but my grip remained resolute.

"Jiro!" Hoka's voice sliced through my turmoil. "Lower your weapon."

My finger hovered over the trigger, the maelstrom of emotions clashing within me.

"You shot at me twelve years ago like I was a rabid dog. I saw those tattoos when your arm came out of the car, and you fired at us, killing Anna." I pointed toward Hope. "*Her* sister. I have every right to take your life."

"I wh—" Valdez raised his hands in surrender. "I didn't know it was you. You weren't even supposed to be there."

"What does that mean?" Hoka's voice broke the tense stillness, pulling me back from the precipice of my anger. His presence was a lifeline, grounding me in a reality that seemed to waver.

I looked around the room, my eyes flicking between Valdez's guarded expression and Hoka's concerned gaze. The only thread of rationality I had left was barely stopping me from pulling that trigger.

The memories surged, vivid and raw. Anna's lifeless form sprawled on the ground, her eyes empty, haunted my thoughts. I could still feel the desperation that had gripped me as I had crawled toward her as the world around me crumbled. And then, out of that chaos, Hoka had emerged like a guardian angel, yanking me away from the brink.

Yet, there was resentment that lingered; part of me had hated him for saving me. It had been easier back then to share my self-loathing with him, to let him bear some of the weight of my guilt. I suspected he understood and accepted the unfair burden of my anger without a word.

But right now, in this room, the ghosts of the past seemed to loom larger than ever. I needed to push back the overwhelming tide of emotion and focus on the present, on the man before me who held answers.

"What do you mean I wasn't supposed to be there?" My voice trembled with anger and pain, the memories flashing before me like shards of glass.

I tempted a look at Hope, and despite the tears in her blue eyes, seeing her there, with her focus on me, took some of the pain away. How was that even possible?

Valdez's posture changed as he threw a look full of

disdain at Leo before concentrating on me again. "I had no clue who you were, nor did I care that a yakuza was present. Those were different times, and I was still acting under my father's command back then."

A heavy silence fell upon the room, the words sinking in like stones dropped into still water. I lowered my gun, my hand shaking slightly, the anger that had fueled me now mixing with disbelief.

Valdez turned his attention toward Leo again, his gaze seething with contempt. "Did you let him carry the weight of *your* mistakes? Do you always like to play the victim?"

Valdez's words pierced through the room, a reckoning that seemed to be long overdue. Leo's face twisted with a blend of guilt and defiance, and he took a step back but was blocked by one of Valdez's men.

"It's not as simple as that!" Leo spat violently. "Yakuza are bad news; one way or another, my sister would have ended up dead! Look at Hope now, tied to a chair!" He pointed at Hope, who was glaring at him despite the tears running down her face.

Valdez snorted, "You're delusional. Your sister being tied to this chair surrounded by armed men is a hundred percent on you." He sighed, his attention returning to me. "Let me enlighten you, yakuza. Back then, Leo was the star quarterback of his high school, so we approached him for a 'partnership.' You see, there's a lot of money in high school and university games. Leo's greed had no end, and he saw this as an opportunity to fuel it even further. He started making deals with other parties, which could have spiraled out of control." Valdez shrugged.

"The sister's death was… unfortunate but necessary. Leo's greed needed to be controlled, and that was the warning he understood," he continued, his tone steady but heavy with the weight of the past. "A message to keep on the straight and narrow. Leo had been warned many times. But it seems his desire for more blindsided him to the dangers."

A shiver ran down my spine as the puzzle pieces began to fit together, revealing a portrait of deceit and manipulation that I had never suspected. I'd never been the one to blame for Anna's death. It was Leo… Leo, whose tears at Anna's funeral were more about the weight of his guilt than genuine sorrow. Leo, who had traded his sister's life as if it were a commodity, cared little for the past they shared.

"Unfortunately, it seems that guilt, or maybe karma, who knows, played its part because, after his sister's death, our Leo was no longer capable of influencing the outcome of a game, but…" Valdez shook his head. "He was good at recognizing desperation and greed in other players like him. He's been our best recruiter."

The selfishness of Leo's actions struck me like a blow.

How easy it must be to carry such a burden without an ounce of remorse or accountability, I thought bitterly, the anger within me surging, threatening to consume reason.

Everything he had done had been for money and not to help his family; no, that would have been somehow commendable. He'd done everything for himself, not caring who died in the process, even his own flesh and blood.

My eyes flicked to Hoka, and he met my gaze with understanding. He saw the storm of resolve and determination forming into a chilling purpose. Leo Myers had to pay, and I would be the one killing him.

The prospect of ending his life didn't cause any issue with my conscience. Sometimes, trees that had grown twisted couldn't be straightened. They only spread their poison, threatening to destroy everything around them. I wouldn't let that darkness taint my Hope's world any longer.

Hope's presence caught my attention. She looked down, her vulnerability exposed, and Oda's comforting touch sparked a flicker of jealousy inside me. That was supposed to be my role—to provide her with solace, to shield her from pain. But right now, my yakuza persona demanded priority. I had to be the guardian, even if it meant pushing my personal feelings aside.

I faced an agonizing truth—I couldn't always choose her, couldn't always put her first, no matter how much I yearned to. This realization added another layer to my unworthiness. Would she understand my decision to eliminate her brother, or would she despise me for it? Could she see beyond the act to the underlying truth—that her safety was paramount to me, even if it meant tearing my own heart apart in the process?

"You don't have a legitimate reason to wage a war, Nishimura."

"Perhaps, but if my *wakagashira* wants to spill blood, I'll stand by him."

Hoka's unwavering support was a lifeline. He was willing to go to battle for me despite the chaos I had inadvertently brought into his life.

"I didn't intend for yakuza bloodshed, and you know the implications of that. And before you cast a stone, take a good look at yourself and tell me you've never used leverage to make a point."

My lips tightened. I couldn't deny it. Both Hoka and I were far from blameless, and we had used collateral in the past.

Valdez's smirk widened. "But you know what, yakuza? I'll grant you the retribution you're after." Before I could inquire about his intentions, Valdez reached behind him, retrieving a gun and shooting Leo Myers in the head.

I stared in shock at the abrupt act.

"He was becoming more trouble than he was worth. Take the girl and leave. Our business here is concluded."

I looked at Hoka, his expression a mask of cool indifference. While it wasn't uncommon for syndicates to sever ties with problematic members, Valdez's swift action left me somewhat stunned. I couldn't predict how Hope would react to this sudden turn of events.

"Go to her; you're who she needs right now," Hoka whispered.

I nodded, each step toward Hope quickening the hammering of my heart. Would she shy away from me? Be repulsed? Would she run to her brother's lifeless body to grieve? My mind raced with uncertainty, but I didn't have long to dwell on it. As Oda finished cutting her ties, Hope removed her gag and rushed directly into my arms.

She clung to me, burying her face in my neck, her silent tears soaking into my skin. The overwhelming relief I felt was impossible to put into words. She wasn't rejecting me; in fact, she sought comfort in my embrace. I wrapped one arm tightly around her back, leaning down to hook my other arm under her knees, lifting her into my arms as she clung to my neck.

Kissing the top of her head, I released a long, grateful breath. Carrying the most precious person in my life, I walked away from those haunting memories. Oda followed us, his usually composed expression now grim, his eyes filled with concern. He opened the car door for us.

"Ikiteru koto yori ai shiteru," *I love you more than life itself,* I whispered into her hair.

Oda shot me a surprised look as I settled into the seat with Hope still on my lap, holding her tightly and gently rubbing her arm.

Hoka joined us in silence, his expression mirroring Oda's concern. Both of them understood how life-altering it could be to witness death in such a brutal manner.

After a few minutes, Hope's breathing deepened, and by the time the car stopped in front of Hoka's hotel, she was fast asleep.

I carefully got out of the car, making sure not to wake her.

"All the emotions must have drained her," Hoka commented, giving her a concerned look. "Take her to the guest room in our suite."

"Thank you," I murmured, brushing my lips against her hair once more. "Sleep, my love. I'll keep you safe."

EIGHTEEN

Hope

I woke up feeling groggy, my senses slowly returning to me. I opened my eyes and found Jiro sleeping beside me, on top of the covers. But unlike the peaceful slumber he'd had after that unforgettable night we'd shared what seemed like a million years ago, his expression was different now. His eyebrows were furrowed, as if even in his sleep, he was deep in thought, worried about everything.

I lay there, silently watching him, feeling a strange numbness inside me. My brother was dead... the only family I had left now resided in a care home with no real recollection of my existence. The weight of my loneliness settled over me like a heavy blanket, making it hard to breathe.

Jiro's eyes fluttered open, and his dark orbs met mine. He didn't speak right away, just stared at me, assessing, as if he could read the cause of my distress.

"Is it weird," I finally found my voice, "that after all he did, after he sold me without a second thought, there's a part of me that will miss him?"

Jiro's gaze remained steady, his dark eyes locked onto mine. "No, it's not weird at all. People are complicated, Hope. There was a time when Leo wasn't the person who betrayed you. That part of him, the one you loved, it's natural to grieve for that too."

I sighed, my breath trembling as I tried to sort through my emotions. Turning onto my back, I stared at the moldings on the hotel room's ceiling.

"I'm sorry for your loss," Jiro said gently.

I nodded, my response muted. "Will he... resurface?" I asked hesitantly.

Jiro lay on his back beside me. "No." And for once, I was grateful he didn't expand on this. He sighed. "And I know I don't really need to say it, but you can never tell anyone what happened. Because, Hope, I will not be able to protect you if you do."

Because you won't be there anymore.

"Don't worry about me, Jiro Saito. I'll live my life on the straight and narrow. You can leave with peace of mind."

I heard his head turn on the pillow, and I could feel his eyes on the side of my face, but I kept looking at the ceiling as if it were the most fascinating thing in the world. I didn't want him to see the turmoil and pain his departure was causing.

"Hope." The softness of his voice stung a little; it felt a lot like pity to me.

"How do you feel knowing you weren't to blame for Anna's death?" I asked, desperately switching the focus from me to him. "That must be a relief."

Jiro didn't respond immediately, and I turned my head toward him. He was facing me, but his eyes were locked on some distant point only he could see.

After a pause, he finally spoke, his voice deeper. "It is a relief. But it's also surreal. After carrying that guilt for so long, it almost feels like I've lost a part of myself."

I couldn't help but feel a twinge of sympathy. "You've carried that responsibility for too long, Jiro. It was a burden that you should never have borne." I forced a little smile. "Now you can finally let it go and leave all this behind." Leave *me* behind.

His eyebrows dipped, his gaze searching mine. "I think we need to discuss this. You're alone here now, and I want—"

I didn't want his pity, not when what I truly craved was his love and commitment. "It's quite freeing, yes, I agree.

Now I can do whatever I want. It's so liberating," I said, with a voice as light as I could muster to mask the pain in my heart.

There was a flicker of something akin to frustration and longing in his eyes, but he didn't say more. Instead, he stood up and motioned toward the en suite bathroom. "There are clean clothes in there. Once you're ready, come out to the main room. Hoka and Violet are waiting."

As he left the room, I couldn't help but feel the weight of uncertainty settling in. Had I just made a mistake?

I waited until I heard the bedroom door close behind him, then slowly rose from the bed. His words echoed in my mind, and I couldn't shake the feeling that I had pushed him away when all I truly wanted was to be closer to him.

I moved to the en suite and turned on the shower, letting the hot water wash over me. It was a blissful sensation, and for a moment, I allowed myself to simply bask in it. But as the water cascaded down my body, I couldn't escape the thoughts that flooded my mind.

Leo is dead. My only family had betrayed me. Sold me without a second thought. Realizing the extent of my loneliness, it hit me like a ton of bricks, and I pressed my forehead against the shower tiles. Silent tears mixed with the water, unnoticed and unseen.

I stayed in the shower longer than necessary, the heat soothing both my body and my troubled thoughts. A part of me had hoped that Jiro would join me like he had done before, wrap his arms around me, kiss the back of my neck, and make all the promises and love declarations I was longing to hear. But that was a distant memory, a foolish dream, a chapter in our lives that had come to a painful close.

"Fool," I muttered as I turned off the water.

I quickly dried off and dressed in the clothes I assumed were Violet's. The flowy royal-blue midi skirt and cream satin shirt were likely the nicest, most luxurious items I had ever worn, and I marveled at how they seemed to transform me into someone different.

I stood in front of the mirror, staring at my reflection as if trying to recognize the woman looking back at me. I took a few deep breaths, steeling myself for what lay ahead. I had faced countless failures, heartbreaks, and disappointments in my life, and this would be no different. I would fake it until I made it, as I always did.

Did you really?

Pushing my doubts aside, I opened the bedroom door and stepped into the main room. Hoka was leaning over Violet, who cradled their son. Despite his fearsome appearance, his eyes held a tenderness I'd never seen before.

"Oh, sorry!" I stammered, stepping back quickly into the room, my heart aching with a surprising pang of longing.

It was possible for a yakuza to be happy, and it was possible for him to make a woman like me happy. He just needed to want it.

"Hope! Come, don't be silly. We're done," she called with laughter.

I opened the door and noticed Hoka now holding their baby. The weight of his gaze almost made me retreat, but Violet's inviting pat on the sofa drew me in.

"I can't thank you enough, Hoka," I said, my voice

thick with emotion.

His eyes shimmered with something unreadable. "That's what families do," he replied softly. "Though I wish things had ended differently."

I nodded. My gaze swept around the room, searching for any sign of Jiro and Oda, but they were conspicuously absent. A knot of unease settled in my stomach, and I couldn't help but ask, "Where are Jiro and Oda?"

Hoka hesitated, sharing a fleeting look with Violet. "They're preparing. We leave for California tonight."

"Tonight…" My heart sank. "Right, yes." That realization hit me harder than I expected. Standing abruptly, I stammered, "I should let you get ready." My scattered thoughts led me to my forgotten bag on the mantel. "I'll return the clothes."

Violet rose, her voice trembling, "Hope, wait—"

But Hoka silenced her with a subtle shake of his head. The finality of that gesture stung.

He wanted me to go too, of course. Why would he spend time with me? I was not part of the family, nor was I ever considered part of it. Jiro's obvious absence said more than words ever could.

My cheeks started to burn with the fake smile I tried to keep despite the rejection I was feeling. You would think I was used to it by now, but it did not hurt any less.

My face warmed as my eyes started to sting with unshed tears. "I've got to go. Lots of work. And don't worry, this"—I gestured vaguely—"never happened."

Reaching the door, I paused. "Tell Jiro and Oda… thanks. For everything."

Violet's eyes glistened, but Hoka replied, "We'll see you soon, Hope."

With a final nod, I slipped out, swallowed by the hall to return to my life.

***

With a steaming latte that cost more than I'd like to admit and a reluctant vow to cover every holiday shift for the coming year, I managed to win back Max's trust after my unexplained two-day absence. His frown softened when I told him Jiro had left and Leo, with all his complications, had decided to move on.

I hardly believed how I could even utter those words without my voice breaking, especially after the harrowing sight of my brother's tragic end just a day ago. Perhaps my heart had already mourned Leo long before, grieving for the brother he once was, not the stranger he had become.

The silence of my apartment was deafening, a stark contrast to the whirlwind of events that had recently unfolded. Every secret was out, every threat neutralized. Yet, in the midst of newfound freedom, an overwhelming sense of loneliness consumed me.

I sank into the worn-out sofa, flipping through a college catalog. Once, the idea of a fresh start, free from the chains of my past, was all I yearned for. But that was before Jiro's return, reigniting a childhood infatuation into a blazing passion.

As if the universe sensed my thoughts, my phone buzzed beside me, Jiro's name lighting up the screen. Glancing at the clock, it was past eight. Was he calling to say goodbye from California?

Torn, I let the phone ring, not ready to face the emotions his voice might stir up.

I took a deep breath, trying to shake off the heaviness that settled in my chest after ignoring Jiro's call. The silence of the apartment was suddenly interrupted by a soft knock on the door. Hesitating for a moment, I approached and opened it to find Jiro standing there, holding a bag of fish tacos.

"I figured you wouldn't answer," he admitted. His voice a soft caress against my senses. "But leaving without seeing you one last time?" His eyes searched mine, looking for any sign of the emotions I was desperately trying to hide. "That's not me."

With my heart in my throat, I stepped aside, allowing him to enter.

As he walked past, he glanced at the college catalog on the table. "Planning for the future?" he asked with a hint of sadness in his voice.

I nodded, trying to find the right words. "I need to figure things out," I whispered, my voice betraying the turmoil inside. "Now that anything is possible." *Anything except a future with you.*

Jiro's gaze intensified, and before I could react, he closed the distance between us. Our lips met in a desperate kiss, filled with longing and unspoken words. The world around us faded as the intensity of our connection took over.

His hands roamed my back, pulling me closer while mine tangled in his hair. The intensity was overwhelming, every touch igniting a fire that threatened to consume us. We moved together, a dance of passion and longing, each touch a silent plea, each kiss a promise.

But as the heat between us grew, Jiro pulled away, his chest heaving. "We shouldn't," he whispered, his voice filled with anguish. "This isn't just a goodbye, Hope. It's an ending."

Tears filled my eyes. "Then let it be a beautiful ending," I murmured, pulling him back to me. "Let's make this night a memory, a testament to what we shared."

I saw hesitation in his eyes for a few seconds as his eyebrows dipped. I was not above begging for a last night together, but before I could speak, I saw it; his control snapped, and the almost animalistic side of him took over. He crashed his lips on mine and grabbed my bottom lip between his teeth, biting gently.

He let his hands roam down my body, grabbing my ass and pulling me up, and as I gasped, he deepened the kiss with a dominance I was more than happy to submit to.

I wrapped my legs around his narrow waist as he walked to the bedroom without breaking the kiss.

He finally broke the kiss as he let me fall on the bed and removed his shirt in the same movement. I stared at his beautiful chest, taking in as much detail of his tattoos as possible, trying to imprint them in my memory.

He kept his eyes on me as he slowly undid his jeans, each movement increasing the desperate pool of desire forming in my lower belly. He lowered them, along with his underwear, and he stood there in front of me, his body utter perfection—hard and defined as if he had been sculpted in marble. His impressive length standing straight, his desire as intense as mine.

Seeing him in all his naked glory sent my heart into overdrive, its rapid beats echoing loudly in my ears. Without hesitation, I shed my own shirt, letting it join the discarded pile on the floor. I was thankful for the forethought to have left the bra behind earlier. With a swift motion, I slid off my yoga pants, leaving nothing between us but the raw intensity of our emotions.

I felt brazen. Powerful. And despite the remaining shyness, I opened my legs wide, showing him the extent of my own desire.

He licked his lips as he joined me on the bed, nestling himself between my legs, spreading me even more to accommodate his hulking body, pressing his hardness right on my overly sensitive clit, and I moaned at the simple contact.

"God, you're breathtaking," he murmured, his lips grazing my cheekbone before continuing a tortuous journey downward. The mix of soft licks and teasing bites sent waves of pleasure across my skin, bringing me to the verge of insanity.

My senses were on hyperdrive. I closed my eyes, wanting to memorize every nuance of this moment. I wanted to remember everything, every single detail. How my body reacted to his licks, his love bites, and gentle caresses. How his calloused fingers felt on my sensitive skin. How his hot skin and heavy body felt on top of me. How his cologne was even more intoxicating mixed with the shared exertions of lovemaking. And how it felt when his hot mouth closed around my nipples or how his tongue felt in my wet heat.

I was determined to hold on to every moment, every

shared breath, every whispered word. Because I knew that after tonight, the memories would be all I had of my time with Jiro Saito.

After making me orgasm on his wicked tongue, he kissed his way back up and stopped for a second to put on a condom.

"Look into my eyes, *koibito*," he said, his voice husky as he positioned himself against my entrance.

I met his gaze, noticing the intense focus in his eyes.

"I want to see all of you when—" He paused, searching my eyes for a hint of hesitation. "When I'm inside you."

His intensity gripped me, holding me captive in the deep pools of his gaze. There was vulnerability there, mixed with desire, an emotion that echoed within my own heart.

I nodded, and he pushed in with torturing slowness until he was in to the hilt. He started to move slowly, and despite our overwhelming desire, he kept his thrusts slow and gentle. He made sweet love to me, whispering sweet words in Japanese as I held on to him, never wanting to let go.

I came again, and he followed quickly behind, and I wanted to weep at the intensity of what we'd just shared. I would never heal from Jiro.

The night was full of tenderness and passion. We explored each other, savoring every touch, every whispered word. It was a dance of love and heartbreak, of two souls trying to hold on to a fleeting moment.

As dawn approached, I nestled into Jiro's embrace, the rhythmic beat of his heart lulling me to sleep.

When I awoke, the bed was empty, but a small box and a note lay on the side table.

Tears filled my eyes as I opened the box to reveal a stunning gold and diamond katana pendant. The note simply read, "I will always be your warrior."

The room was filled with the echoes of our last night together, a bittersweet reminder of a love that was both profound and heartbreaking.

NINETEEN

Jiro

The California sun was a stark contrast to the memories that clouded my mind. The life I had left behind two years ago as Hoka's *wakagashira* was familiar, like an old song you can't help but hum along to. But even amid the familiarity, there was an emptiness, a void that seemed to grow with each passing day.

Hope.

She was everywhere, in every shadow, every whisper of the wind, every dream that took me away in the depths of the night. She was a ghost, not of the past, but of a future that could have been. A future where love wasn't sacrificed for duty, where choices weren't made out of obligation.

The garden was my sanctuary, a place where I could lose myself in thoughts and memories. The scent of blooming flowers. The gentle rustling of leaves. It all brought a semblance of peace.

Hoka's presence was silent but strong as he took a seat beside me. We sat in silence, two old friends lost in their own worlds. The weight of his gaze was palpable, and I knew he had something to say.

"I've missed you, Jiro," Hoka began. His voice soft, filled with genuine emotion. "Not just as my *wakagashira*, but as my brother, my confidant."

I turned to look at him, meeting his earnest eyes. "I've missed this too," I admitted. "But there's a part of me that's still back there, with her."

Hoka sighed, running a hand through his hair. "I see it, you know. The way you look off into the distance, the way your face changes when you think of her. Hope has left an indelible mark on you."

I swallowed hard, the lump in my throat making it difficult to speak. "I left to protect her, to give her a chance at a normal life."

Hoka's gaze was unwavering. "But did you ever give

her the choice? Did you ever think that maybe, just maybe, she wanted a life with you, regardless of the complications?"

His words hit me like a ton of bricks. Had I been so blinded by my sense of duty that I never considered what Hope truly wanted?

"She deserves better," I whispered, my voice breaking.

Hoka placed a reassuring hand on my shoulder. "Maybe she does. But she also deserves a say in her own life. And maybe, just maybe, she chooses you."

The weight of his words settled in, and for the first time in weeks, a glimmer of hope stirred inside me.

Hoka's gaze softened, a vulnerability peeking through that I had rarely seen. "If you want to leave and be with her, I wouldn't blame you," he said, his voice sincere.

I scoffed, finding it hard to believe. Hoka, with his unwavering dedication to our legacy, contemplating leaving it all behind? It seemed impossible.

He caught my disbelief and chuckled softly. "I did, Jiro. When I thought I was going to lose Violet, I offered to leave everything. And I meant every word."

I looked at him, taken aback. Hoka and Violet's love story was legendary within our circles, but I never realized the depth of his feelings. "You would have given up the legacy? Just like that?"

Hoka nodded, his eyes distant as he remembered. "Violet is my world. Choosing her, choosing *us*, was the only choice that made sense. Our legacy, our duty, it means nothing if you don't have someone to share it with."

I felt a pang in my heart, thinking of Hope. The nights we shared, the dreams we built, all of it came rushing back.

Hoka seemed to sense my turmoil. "Listen, Jiro," he began, his voice firm, "If you want to bring her here, to our home. She is most welcome, and I know Violet is eager to have another woman here with her, but if you want to be in Seattle with her, I can put you in charge there. I could use a man like you in Seattle. If you decide to leave to be with her, there will be no hard feelings. Only understanding."

I let out a deep sigh, the weight of my past influencing any decision. "It's not that simple, Hoka. I was her sister's boyfriend, and when I knew her, she was merely a child. It feels like… I shouldn't feel the way I feel."

Hoka looked at me for a second before turning toward the pond again. "You were. But that feels like a lifetime ago. Times change, Jiro. People change. I changed, and I know you did, too. We were what, twenty-one at the time? Fuck, we knew nothing about the men we would become."

I turned to him, grappling with the little line of hope he was throwing my way. "Do you really believe it could work? After everything? There was a time when I believed it could work with Anna, too. Until she demanded I change, and the fight caused her to be at the wrong place at the wrong time. I will not make the same mistake with Hope. She is my heart and soul. If she ended up resenting this life, resenting me… I don't think I could survive."

"Then let her in. Be honest with her. Trust her to make the right decision for herself. But don't push her away out of fear. That's not fair to either of you."

I met his gaze. "I love her, Hoka. More than I've ever loved anyone. And the thought of losing her, of her getting hurt because of me… it terrifies me."

"She's your *ikigai*, isn't she?"

The term *ikigai*, a Japanese concept meaning "a reason for being," struck a chord deep within me. I fought it with all my might, but I had lost, and I had to admit it to myself and to both of us.

I nodded. "Yes, she is," I admitted with finality.

Hoka clapped a hand on my shoulder, his grip firm and reassuring. "Then trust in that. Our ancestors have a way of guiding us. They don't make mistakes. I doubted them once and almost destroyed my relationship with the love of my life. Don't do that. Hope deserves to have a say in her own future. And if she chooses you, then you owe it to her and to yourself to fight for that love. No matter the cost." He let out a low chuckle. "Speaking of the love of my life, Violet wanted me to share her brother's story with Lily."

The realization dawned on me, and I couldn't help but smirk. "Violet put you up to this, didn't she?"

Hoka laughed, his eyes shining with amusement. "Of course she did. She's the heart and soul of our family, always looking out for everyone, and she worries about you and Hope."

I leaned back on the bench, a wry smile playing on my lips. Violet was giving me far more consideration than I deserved. "Considering she's not my biggest fan, that's quite the gesture." And I couldn't blame her for it either. I cost her… *them* so much. I would hate me if I were her.

You already do.

"Quite the contrary, actually. My wife likes you; even when I was ready to throw you off a cliff, she saw something in you." He waved his hand dismissively. "She is a bottomless well of goodness and forgiveness. Something that allowed me to get her back but that I can't really turn off whenever I please. She wants you happy and she thinks you have walked away from Hope too fast. She wanted to meddle that day at the hotel, and maybe I should have let her."

"Maybe so," I muttered, feeling like an inept teenager needing his mother's assistance. I sighed, rubbing the back of my neck. "I've given her plenty of reasons to think otherwise."

Hoka leaned in, his voice dropping to a conspiratorial whisper. "Between you and me, she's got a soft spot for lost causes. Take Alessandro Benetti, for instance."

I frowned. "What's the story there?"

Hoka rolled his eyes. "You won't get the flowery version Violet likes to give. Basically, Sandro was a moron, thinking Lily was better without him, which made them both miserable. Violet, being Violet, intervened. And by 'intervened,' I mean she literally kicked his ass."

I chuckled. "Metaphorically?"

Hoka smirked, tapping his temple. "Nope, and it's a memory I'll cherish forever. Anyway, once he pulled his head out of his ass, he went back to her, and they are happy now."

I took a deep breath, my thoughts drifting back to Hope. "You think she's miserable? Hope, I mean?"

Hoka looked at me like I was the dumbest person to have ever existed. "You must know she loves you."

"She said that much, but it was in bed after—" I cleared my throat. "We don't really think clearly in those moments."

Hoka snorted. "No, we certainly don't. But women…" He shook his head. "They know their feelings. If she said the words, she meant them, and she was miserable when she realized you were not in the hotel room."

I swallowed hard, the weight of his words sinking in. "But this life… it's not easy."

Hoka shook his head, exasperated. "She's not in love with the life, Jiro. She's in love with you. Everything else is just background noise."

"I just—"

"Go speak with Violet," Hoka offered suddenly. "Honestly, just go. She sent me, but I'm so shit at this I'm set up to fail. She'll have the right words."

I couldn't help but smile. "You're not doing so bad."

"For real?" he asked quite cheerfully.

I laughed. "No, you're terrible, but then so am I, so I understood what you meant." I sighed and stood up. "I think I need to take a trip to Seattle."

Hoka mirrored my movement and stood as well. "The plane is ready and waiting for you."

I arched an eyebrow. "How did you know I would go?"

It was Hoka's turn to laugh now. "I may not be the most articulate when it comes to matters of the heart, but I know men like us. I know how obsessively we love."

***

The soft hum of a lullaby led me to the nursery, where I found Violet, her silhouette framed by the soft glow of the room's window. She was gently rocking her son nestled in her arms, his tiny fingers wrapped around hers. The sight was heartwarming, a stark contrast to the world we lived in.

She looked up, her eyes brightening with a warm smile. "Jiro," she greeted, her voice a soft whisper so as not to disturb the baby. "What brings you here?"

I hesitated, taking a moment to gather my thoughts. "I've been wondering… have you ever regretted this life? Being part of the yakuza, living by its rules?"

Violet paused, her gaze drifting to her son, then back to me. "Not for a single day," she replied with conviction. "Yes, there's darkness in this life, and I've felt its weight firsthand. But the love, the joy, the moments like these"—she gestured to the cradle—"they make it all worth it."

I took a deep breath, my insecurities bubbling to the surface. "I'm not sure I'm worthy of Hope. I've made countless mistakes, Violet. Big ones."

Violet's gaze softened, her maternal instincts shining through. "It's those very doubts, Jiro, that make you worthy. It means you care. That you want to be better for her."

I looked down, struggling to swallow past the lump of emotion lodged in my throat. "But what if I can't give her the life she deserves?"

Violet chuckled softly, her eyes twinkling with mischief. "Hope reminds me so much of myself when I first joined Hoka. She's strong, resilient, and fiercely loyal. She'll be an incredible partner for you, and together, you'll build a beautiful life here."

I smiled, feeling a weight lift off my shoulders. "Thank you. That means more than you know."

She grinned, her playful side emerging. "Plus, I can already see Hope and I becoming fast friends. We need more strong women around here. It's about time we balance out all this testosterone."

I laughed, the tension in the room dissipating. "I'll drink to that."

Violet winked, her mood lightening. "Just remember, Jiro, love is a journey. And with Hope by your side, it's a journey worth taking."

I hesitated, my fingers drumming on the edge of the crib. "I'm heading to Seattle soon," I admitted, my voice barely above a whisper. "It's been three weeks since I last spoke to Hope. I'm… I'm worried about how she'll receive me."

Violet gently placed her son in the crib, ensuring he was snug and comfortable. She then turned to face me, her eyes searching mine. "Jiro," she began, her voice soft yet firm, "when I ran away from Hoka, when I was at my lowest, wishing I could just disappear, even when I tried to convince myself I hated him… deep down, I always loved him."

I swallowed hard, her words resonating with the turmoil within me.

She continued, "There's this inexplicable connection, a pull that's impossible to resist. It's the *ikigai*, I'm sure of it. Before I even knew what it meant, I felt it with Hoka. And I'm certain Hope feels the same about you."

I looked down, my heart heavy with hope and fear. "But what if she doesn't want this life here? What if it's too much to ask?"

Violet stepped closer, placing a comforting hand on my arm. "Then you'll know. But you won't know unless you try. Go to her, Jiro. Be honest. Lay your heart bare, share your feelings, your fears, your doubts. Let her show *you* that, in the grand scheme of things, they matter so little compared to the love you share."

I nodded, taking a deep breath. "Thank you, Violet. I needed to hear that."

She smiled, her eyes warm and understanding. "Sometimes, all we need is a little push in the right direction. Now go and bring Hope back into your life."

I stepped out of the house, the cool evening air brushing against my face. The sleek black car awaited me, its engine purring softly. Sliding into the back seat, I drummed my fingers on my leg, my mind racing with thoughts of Hope.

"Okay, Jiro," I muttered to myself, trying to rehearse what I'd say to her. "Hope, from the moment I saw you again, my heart… um, did that thing. You know, the fluttery thing. And I realized… um, that you're like… the peanut butter to my jelly?"

I groaned, slapping my forehead. "That's terrible."

I tried again, attempting to sound more poetic. "Hope, you're the moonlight in my darkest nights, the… um, sugar in my coffee?"

I could almost hear Oda's mocking laughter in my head. "Really, Jiro? Sugar in your coffee? Typical millennial," he'd mutter, shaking his head in mock disappointment.

I sighed as the driver pulled onto the main road that led to the airfield. The city lights blurred past me, but all I could think of was Hope. "Come on, Jiro," I pep-talked myself. "You've faced down dangerous men, navigated the treacherous world of the yakuza, you know how to kill a man a hundred and twenty-two different ways, and yet you can't string together a simple love confession?"

I imagined Oda beside me, smirking. "It's always the tough ones who struggle with matters of the heart," he'd say, chuckling.

I rolled my eyes, even though Oda wasn't really there. "Thanks for the pep talk," I muttered sarcastically.

As the airfield came into view, I took a deep breath, trying to calm my racing heart. "Okay, one last try," I whispered to myself. "Hope, from the moment I laid eyes on you, my world shifted. You're the missing piece I never knew I was searching for. I love you, and I'll do whatever it takes to make you see that."

It wasn't perfect, but it was honest. And as the car parked and I headed toward the waiting plane, I hoped it would be enough.

As I settled into the plush seat of the plane, the engines roared to life, and we began our ascent. I closed my eyes, took a deep breath, and whispered a silent prayer, "Ancestors, grant me one last wish, one last shot at heaven. Let me keep my literal and proverbial Hope—that vibrant five-foot-two woman with purple hair and eyes so blue, I could drown in them and die with a smile on my face." The plane soared higher, taking my hopes and prayers with it.

TWENTY

Hope

The soft hum of the emporium's air conditioning was the only sound that filled the space. The dim lighting cast a sultry glow over the shelves lined with an array of intimate products. It was a quiet day, with only a few customers drifting in and out, leaving me with more time than I'd like to be alone with my thoughts.

I was in the back room, restocking and organizing when my mind began to wander to Jiro. The quietness of the shop only amplified the emptiness I felt without him. Three weeks had passed, and the sting of his absence hadn't dulled, and I had yet to figure out what I truly wanted to do with my life.

I should have just moved on; we'd been together not even a full month. It meant nothing in the grand scheme of things.

I snorted as I aligned the fruit-flavored lubricants on the bottom shelves. Come to think of it, Jiro had been gone almost as long as he'd been here, and I was still the stupid ten-year-old pining for him.

He had certainly moved on, back to his life as Hoka's second-in-command, back to being the feared, powerful figure he was born to be. Where would a lost girl from Seattle fit in all of this? Nowhere. That much was clear from the painful silence.

Oda had been texting, joking, and being his carefree self now that he was back in Chicago, too far from Jiro to offer me any reassurance that the heartbreak was maybe mutual. But from Jiro? Nothing. It was as if he'd vanished, leaving me to deal with all the emotions he had awakened in me. The silence from his end was deafening, making me question the authenticity of everything we shared. Was it possible for such passion to simply evaporate?

The soft chime of the doorbell pulled me from my sullen reverie, and I stepped out of the back room, ready to assist the customer. My heart stopped when I saw him.

Jiro.

He was standing there, looking around the shop with a casual interest, his hands buried in the pockets of his black dress pants.

For a moment, I thought I was dreaming. The pain of the past weeks made this moment feel surreal.

I shook my head and blinked a few times; if it was a dream, I had to wake up now because if I didn't, the wake-up call promised to be painful.

He smiled as he saw the katana hanging from my neck. As he took a couple of steps inside, he caught my eye, and with a playful smirk, he said, "Hey, I'm looking for some new nipple rings. My girlfriend has this thing for them," he added, winking, pretending not to recognize me.

I felt a thrill run through me, realizing he was referring to me as his girlfriend.

Playing along, I approached him with a professional demeanor and stepped behind the counter. "Of course, sir. We have a variety of designs. Any particular style you're interested in?" I added, gesturing to the selection under the glass.

He leaned in, his voice dropping to a seductive whisper. "Something that'll drive her wild when she sees them… and licks them."

I felt the uncomfortable weight of lust settle in my lower belly as my underwear became wet with the arousal that his mere suggestion caused. I was so addicted to him.

I bit my lip, trying to suppress a moan that was building, and pressed my legs together. His eyes flipped down, not missing the movement.

"Well, we have these new designs that just came in. They're quite… tantalizing." I showed him a set, our fingers brushing as I handed them over.

He examined them closely, then looked up at me with those intense eyes. "Do you think she'll like them?"

"I have a feeling she'll love them," I replied, my voice quivering slightly.

"Ummm… I think I will get them."

"I can also suggest a set that adapts to piercings in more *private* areas," I added with a blush. "I'm sure she would enjoy the new feelings both in her mouth and in her…"

Jiro leaned a little more over the counter. "Pussy? Is that what you mean?"

I took a sharp intake of breath. Having him talk dirty turned me into a puddle of want, and I knew that if he wanted to, I'd let him take me right there, on this glass counter, and everything else be damned.

There was a charged silence between us, the playful banter giving way to the undeniable chemistry we shared.

"I wonder," he began, his voice husky, "do you think she misses the man who introduced her to such… pleasures?"

I leaned in, my breath catching. "She misses him. Every single day."

Unable to resist any longer, Jiro grabbed the back of my head and closed the distance between us across the counter.

The instant our lips touched, everything else faded away. This wasn't just a kiss; it was an outpouring of weeks filled with longing, silent tears in the night, and dreams where he was just out of reach. Jiro's lips were both tender and demanding, telling a story of love, loss, and reunion.

I melted into him, deepening the kiss, letting it convey everything words had failed to express.

Every moment of heartache, every tear shed in solitude, was washed away in the intensity of our embrace. His taste, a familiar blend of coffee and something I suspected was only his, was intoxicating, pulling me deeper into the whirlwind of emotions.

This kiss was a combination of love and desire, a promise of a future that was to come. It spoke of nights I'd lain awake, yearning for this very touch, and days where memories of him haunted every corner of my mind.

When we finally broke apart, both of us panting slightly, our eyes met in a shared moment of mischief. Jiro's eyes twinkled with that familiar, playful glint I'd come to adore. Without warning, he scooped me up, effortlessly lifting me over the counter. I landed with a soft thud right in front of him, our bodies a breath apart.

"Jiro!" I exclaimed, feigning shock, but my laughter betrayed me. "You're going to give me a heart attack one of these days!"

His fingers danced lightly on my back, pulling me closer. "Only if it means I get to resuscitate you," he teased, his voice dripping with playful seduction.

I rolled my eyes, trying to suppress my grin. "Always the charmer, aren't you?"

He leaned in, his forehead resting against mine, the playful atmosphere replaced with a palpable tension. "Hope," he whispered, his voice husky, sending shivers down my spine. "I've missed you."

It was strange, but the way he said my name as a prayer

allowed me to know everything I had been too scared to hope for. Jiro Saito loved me, too.

My fingers brushed against his warm cheek, the sheer intensity of my emotions causing them to tremble. The joy bubbling up inside me was so overwhelming that, for a moment, I feared this might all be a dream.

"Is it really you?" I whispered, my voice choked with emotion.

He turned his face, pressing a gentle kiss to the center of my palm. "Yes," he murmured, his voice thick with regret. "I'm so sorry I kept you waiting."

Tears welled up, blurring my vision as I gazed into his eyes. "Waiting for what?"

He took a deep breath, his eyes reflecting a depth of emotion that words could hardly capture. "For me to understand what my heart recognized long ago."

"And what is that?"

He gave me a half smile, keeping me tightly in his arms. "I'm a man of action, Hope Myers. I don't want to tell you. I want to show you."

I leaned back in his embrace, now intrigued, and despite the joyful look on his face, I didn't miss the apprehension radiating from him.

"Okay…" I trailed off. "You know there are security cameras here, so if what you want to *show* me is your peen, there's a high probability you'll end up on a certain website."

He chuckled, the sound deep and rich. "The viewer would probably say, 'Lucky girl.'"

I laughed, the sound bubbling up from deep within. I really felt like a lucky girl when I was in his arms. "They'd be right."

He pulled me close again, his eyes serious. "When is your shift finishing?"

I glanced at the clock, momentarily disoriented by the whirlwind of emotions. "In an hour. Max is taking over for the evening."

A slow, promising smile spread across Jiro's face. "Wait for me out front." He leaned down, capturing my lips in a brief but electrifying kiss that left me breathless. "I missed you, *koibito*."

"I missed you, my warrior."

The final hour of my shift at the emporium felt like the longest of my life. Every glance at the clock and every chime of the doorbell heightened my anticipation. Jiro was back. And not just back in town, but back for *me*. Even though he hadn't uttered those three words, his every action, every stolen glance, screamed of unspoken confessions. He loved me. I could feel it.

I tried to distract myself by rearranging some items, but my thoughts kept drifting back to him.

As soon as Max walked in, I almost skipped to the back room, quickly grabbing my bag. Taking a deep breath to calm my racing heart, I stepped outside. There he was, leaning against a sleek car, looking every bit the dashing figure I'd dreamed of during our time apart. The moment our eyes met, the world seemed to blur out, leaving just the two of us.

He pushed off the car, closing the distance between us, and without a word, he pulled me into his embrace, his lips meeting mine in a soft, lingering kiss that spoke of longing and reunion.

Breaking away, he opened the car door for me, and soon we were driving through winding roads, getting out of the city. He gripped my hand, interlacing our fingers and resting our intertwined hands on my lap.

Before I knew it, we pulled up to a picturesque house with a white picket fence. The distant sound of waves crashing against the shore added to the dreamlike atmosphere.

Jiro quickly came around, opening my door and extending his hand. As I took it, the warmth of his grip enveloped me, grounding me in the surreal moment.

"Whose place is this?" My voice was barely above a whisper, the beauty of the scene before me taking my breath away.

He paused, taking a deep breath, his eyes never leaving mine. "Ours, if you'd like it to be."

My heart raced as I searched his eyes, looking for any sign that he might be joking. But all I saw was pure, unfiltered emotion. My voice wavered, disbelief evident in my tone. "You'd really give up everything? Just… us?"

He gently pressed my hand to his lips, his eyes shimmering with emotion. "In a heartbeat, Hope. Without a second thought."

"Jiro, no." His face fell, and I felt a pang of panic, realizing how my response might have sounded. "Jiro, I didn't mean…" He started to pull away, but I tightened my grip, not ready to let go. "I want this. I want us. But I fell for Jiro Saito, the man who took on the world without flinching. I don't want you to change for me."

He frowned, visibly confused.

"But I want to be with you, Jiro Saito. Not a watered-down version you think I need. I love the fearless man. I have nothing keeping me here. I'm sure they have good centers there for Mom and…" I shrugged. "If you don't mind me being there with your family."

"You would move to Hoka's estate with me?"

A smile tugged at my lips. "Yes. It might sound crazy, but from the moment our eyes met, something inside me just… knew. It's hard to put into words."

His eyes softened, filled with understanding. "I feel it, too."

He leaned in, his voice a soft caress against my ear. "*Aishiteru*," he whispered, the Japanese words for *I love you*, sending shivers down my spine. He pulled back slightly, his gaze intense. "I love you, Hope."

Euphoria bubbled up inside me, and I pulled him into a passionate kiss, pouring all my emotions into it. Pulling back slightly, I whispered, "I love you, too."

His smile was radiant. "I can't wait to start the rest of our lives together. I promise, every day, to make sure you never regret choosing me."

The weight of his words, the promise in his eyes, it was all so overwhelming. "I can't wait either," I murmured, a thought crossing my mind. Maybe, just maybe, Anna had a hand in this. Maybe she was the force that brought Jiro and me together, ensuring we found our way to each other.

Jiro's gaze lingered on me, a hint of hesitation in his eyes. "Hope, would it be alright if I stayed with you for the next few days? Until you're ready to come with me?"

I winced slightly, thinking of my modest apartment,

which was nothing compared to the grandeur of the house we'd just left. "You really want to stay at my place? It's not exactly… luxurious."

He stepped closer, cupping my face gently. "Now that I have you, I don't want to spend a single night away from you if I can help it."

His words warmed my heart, and I nodded, a smile playing on my lips. "Alright, but don't say I didn't warn you."

Once we were back, I began to pack, feeling Jiro's gaze on me the entire time. Every so often, he'd come over to help, folding clothes or packing away trinkets. The domesticity of the scene was so heartwarming it felt like we'd been doing this for years.

After a while, I felt his arms wrap around me from behind, pulling me into a gentle embrace. "You okay?" he murmured into my hair before kissing the back of my neck.

I leaned back into him, relishing the warmth and security of his hold. "More than okay. Just… overwhelmed, in the best way."

He turned me around to face him, his eyes searching mine. "Let's take a break," he suggested, leading me to the bedroom.

We both stripped but were too tired to have sex. Just being in his warm embrace, feeling his naked skin against mine, filled me with contentment I had never experienced.

His fingers traced gentle patterns on my back, every touch laced with tenderness.

I rested my head on his chest as Jiro began to describe the property in more detail.

"The estate is huge. There's a main house, of course, but there's also a two-bedroom summerhouse that we'll be sharing. It's nestled right by the sea, so every morning, we'll wake up to the sound of waves crashing."

I propped myself up on one elbow, looking down at him, caressing his tattooed chest. "That sounds amazing. But tell me more about this summerhouse."

He chuckled, his fingers tracing the curve of my cheek. "It's a beautiful place. Traditional Spanish architecture with a touch of modern design. There's a garden that leads right to the beach. I usually spend my early mornings there, practicing martial arts or just meditating by the sea."

I smirked, letting my fingers wander down his chest. "And what if I want to distract you from your morning routines?"

Jiro's eyes darkened with a hint of playfulness. "Well, I've always believed in the importance of... flexibility in one's schedule."

I leaned down, kissing his pierced nipple. "Good, because I plan on being very distracting."

He pulled me closer, his voice dropping to a sultry whisper. "I'm counting on it."

We both chuckled, the playful banter adding a spark to the already palpable chemistry between us.

The dim light of the room played on our skin, casting a soft, intimate glow. "The summerhouse, the estate, it all sounds like a dream," I whispered, my fingers teasingly tracing a path down his torso, finally wrapping around his growing arousal. His sharp intake of breath was music to my ears. "But honestly, as long as I'm with you, it doesn't matter where we are."

Jiro's eyes, dark with desire, locked onto mine, his fingers digging into my waist. "Hearing you say that… You can't even begin to understand how much it means to me." His voice was husky, filled with emotion and raw need. His thumb started to trace circles on my hip, causing goose bumps on my skin. "I promise, Hope, every moment with me will be one you won't forget. And… I intend to keep you thoroughly distracted."

Unable to resist any longer, I captured his lips with mine, the kiss deepening as I positioned myself above him. Slowly, I guided him inside, our combined gasps echoing in the room. With each movement, we lost ourselves in the rhythm, the raw intensity of our connection evident in every shared moan and whispered promise.

We came quickly, a culmination of pent-up desire and weeks of yearning. As we rode the waves of pleasure, we clung to each other, our breaths ragged and hearts racing. In the afterglow, we lay close, sharing whispered dreams and playful jabs about the little things we'd missed about each other.

Nestled against him, the rhythmic beat of his heart beneath my ear was a soothing lullaby. As the edges of sleep began to blur my thoughts, a profound realization settled within me.

Jiro Saito, with those soul-searching eyes, unwavering loyalty, and a heart that loved with a fiery passion, was mine. The weight of our shared past, the challenges we'd faced, and the love we'd discovered all culminated in this beautiful present.

Together, we would write our story, and I couldn't wait to see where our journey would take us.

EPILOGUE

Jiro

Four months.

It's incredible how time can reshape a life. The summerhouse, which once felt like a mere structure of bricks and wood, had transformed into a sanctuary, a home. And it was all because of Hope.

Every evening, as I'd drive back from the estate, the anticipation of seeing her would bubble up inside me. The way she'd infused every corner of our home with her essence was nothing short of magical. The soft glow of the fairy lights she'd hung on the patio, the scent of her favorite lavender candles wafting through the rooms, and the sound of her laughter echoing in the hallways made the summerhouse come alive.

Mornings, though, were a different challenge altogether. Extracting myself from the warmth of our bed, from the cocoon of her arms, was a herculean task. The soft press of her lips against my shoulder. Her gentle murmurs urging me to stay just a few minutes more made every sunrise a battle between duty and desire. I finally understood those knowing looks Hoka used to give me when he talked about Violet. The ones that said, "You'll understand one day." And damn, did I understand now.

Hoka never missed an opportunity to tease me about it. "Look at Jiro," he'd chuckle, "completely wrapped around Hope's little finger." And the truth was, I couldn't even argue because it was true. Every smirk, every joke about me being *whipped,* was met with a proud nod. Because if being utterly and irrevocably in love with Hope meant I was whipped, then so be it.

In these four months, I'd learned that love wasn't just about grand gestures or passionate nights. It was about the quiet moments, the shared dreams, the mutual respect, and the unwavering support. It was about coming home to someone who made every challenge worth facing.

As I stood on the balcony, watching the sun dip below

the horizon, a pair of arms wrapped around me from behind. Hope kissed my back, her breath warm against my skin.

"Lost in thoughts?" she whispered.

"Just thinking about how lucky I am," I replied, turning around to pull her into a tight embrace.

She smiled, her eyes reflecting the last rays of the setting sun. "Me too, my warrior. Me too."

I kissed the top of her head. "How's Yuko?"

She rested her head against my chest. "He's good. He's asleep. Hoka and Violet just needed some alone time tonight. She asked me if I could keep him. You don't mind, do you?"

I let my hands roam down her body and squeezed her shapely ass. "You know I don't. I love the kid. But they don't need that to get it on. I'm sure they just wanted him out so they could do it on every flat surface of the house." I chuckled. "I swear they're going to have triplets by how hard they're trying to get pregnant again."

She laughed, and hearing the melodic sound filled my heart with so much happiness and love I was surprised it was still in my chest. I was ready to do anything to hear it, and I didn't care how silly. I liked doing it.

"You know that's not how it works, right?"

I shrugged, kissing her lips.

"Even if it is the case. They need to do that now. Alessandro and Lily are coming next week with their son, so their privacy will be gone for a while. Oda is coming, too. I offered him the guest room."

"I see we're going from baby to angsty teenager," I joked.

"Oda is older than me."

I rolled my eyes.

She kissed my chest through my shirt. "Plus, I don't mind having Yuko here. It's good practice for when we have our own."

The thought was both exhilarating and terrifying. The idea of little feet running around our home, of Hope cradling a tiny version of us, was something I hadn't allowed myself to fully imagine. But now, with her words hanging in the air, the picture was vivid and, oh, so tempting.

She looked up, her blue eyes searching mine, probably sensing the whirlwind of emotions inside me. "Too soon?" she asked with a playful smirk, her fingers tracing patterns on my chest.

I cleared my throat, trying to find my voice. "No, not too soon. Just... unexpected. But a good kind of unexpected." I paused, taking a deep breath. "I've dreamed of a family with you, Hope. Of us teaching our kids to ride bikes, of family vacations, of bedtime stories. It's just... hearing you say it out loud makes it feel more real."

She giggled, her nose crinkling in that adorable way I loved. "Well, Mr. Saito, if you play your cards right, you might get your wish sooner than you think."

I raised an eyebrow, intrigued. "Is that a promise or a challenge?"

She leaned in, her lips brushing against mine. "Why not both?"

We both laughed, the sound echoing in the evening air. The world seemed to fade away, leaving just the two of us lost in our shared dreams and hopes for the future.

Pulling back slightly, she rested her forehead against mine. "You know, Jiro, every day with you feels like a dream. And if this is what our future looks like, then I can't wait to live every moment of it."

I smiled, my heart swelling with love. "Neither can I, my love. Neither can I."

As the evening deepened and the stars began to twinkle, I held Hope close, her steady heartbeat a comforting rhythm against my chest. The past had been a tumultuous storm, filled with regrets, shadows, and ghosts that haunted my every step. But in allowing myself to face those demons, to seek forgiveness and find redemption, I had discovered a peace I never thought possible.

Hope shifted in my arms, her fingers tracing lazy patterns on my chest. Every touch, every whispered word, was a testament to the love we shared. She was my anchor, my guiding star, the balm that soothed my wounded soul. With her, the weight of the past felt lighter, the future brighter.

I looked down at her, her eyes reflecting the moonlight, and a profound sense of gratitude washed over me. She was my solace, my refuge. Hope, my lover, my heart, my everything. And soon, she would be my wife, the woman I'd build a life with, the mother of our children.

The ghosts of the past had been laid to rest, and in their place stood a future filled with promise and love. With Hope by my side, I was ready to embrace every moment, every challenge, every joy. For she was my everything, and together, we would write our own story, one filled with love, laughter, and endless possibilities.

EPILOGUE

Hope

One year later

The delicate rays of the early morning sun streamed through the sheer curtains, casting a gentle glow across the room. I sat on the balcony, nestled amid lush green plants, a hot cup of tea warming my hands. Lost in the serenity of the moment, my gaze kept drifting to the shimmering wedding ring on my finger and the subtle but growing curve of my belly.

At just four months pregnant, the baby bump was becoming more prominent, a gentle reminder of the life Jiro and I had created together.

Thinking about our unborn child brought a flood of dreams, hopes, and a touch of humor. Would our baby inherit Jiro's stubbornness or my knack for mischief? Would they become a future yakuza boss or take after me and have a penchant for arts and crafts? The very thought of Jiro teaching our child martial arts while I lobbied for painting classes brought a smile to my face. What a fusion of worlds our child was going to experience.

Violet and I became tight, bonding over secrets and countless laughs. The city was full of opportunities, and I jumped into some classes to see what I could learn. Life was buzzing, and I felt anchored by love and purpose.

A gentle touch interrupted my musings. I didn't need to turn to know that Jiro was behind me. His presence always so palpable. The warmth of his hands curved around my waist, fingers tracing tender patterns over the gentle bump that sheltered our growing child.

"You seem miles away," he murmured, his voice deep, tinged with playful curiosity.

"Just daydreaming about whether our little one will be breaking hearts with martial arts moves or with poetic verses," I teased, turning to look up into his eyes.

Jiro chuckled, his eyes twinkling with mirth. "Why not both?"

A mischievous smile played on his lips as he leaned down to capture mine in a soft, lingering kiss filled with promise and passion. The world seemed to pause, the heat of his touch making me forget everything but the man in front of me.

Pulling away slightly, his gaze dropped to our baby bump. With a gentleness that always took me by surprise, he bent to kiss it, his lips warm against my skin.

"Every time I do this," he whispered, sending a shiver down my spine, "I'm reminded of the miracle we've created."

His fingers traced circles on my back, and I leaned into his embrace, savoring the closeness. "Every challenge, every hurdle," he continued, "it was all worth it. For this moment. For our family."

Giggling, I replied, "Let's just hope our child inherits your discipline and not my tendency to binge on chocolate at midnight."

Jiro laughed, the sound rich and full. "Either way, our child will be perfect."

Our laughter and love filled the air, intertwining with the morning light. Creating memories that would last a lifetime.

The End

ABOUT R.G. ANGEL

I'm a trained lawyer, world traveler, coffee addict, cheese aficionado, avid book reviewer and blogger.

I enjoy writing darkish contemporary romance with heart, heat and a little darkness with strong 'morally grey' alpha heroes and strong heroines.

When I'm not busy doing all my lawyerly mayhem, and because I'm living in rainy (yet beautiful) Britain, I mostly enjoy indoor activities such as reading, watching TV, playing with my crazy puppies and writing stories I hope will make you dream and will bring you as much joy as I had writing them.

If you want to know any of the latest news join my reader group R.G.'s Angels on Facebook or subscribe to my newsletter!

Keep calm and read on!

R.G. Angel

ALSO BY

R. G. Angel

The Patricians series
Bittersweet Legacy
Bittersweet Revenge
Bittersweet Truth

The Cosa Nostra series
The Dark King (Prequel Novella)
Broken Prince
Twisted Knight
Cruel King

The Syndicates series
Her Ruthless Warrior
Her Heartless Savior
Her Merciless Protector

Standalones
Lovable
The Tragedy of Us
The Bargain
Hades' Game
The Mistake

Printed in Great Britain
by Amazon